Naomi Patterson

Death By Catgut

Naomi Patterson

Pyewacket Press
New Braunfels, TX 78130

Manufactured in the United States of America.

ISBN 13: 978 – 0615762579
Library of Congress Control Number – 2013902089

Death By Catgut
Acknowledgements

With deep and abiding love, I thank Maureen Nowotny, my sister by birth, Peggy Preiss and Judy Corey, my sisters by choice, for keeping me alive through the dark days.

Writing this book became my ladder out of despair. I want to add a special thank you to Barbara O'Connor and Noreen Means who taught me how to climb while my hands were holding on to my heart.

For the countless chapter reads and edits they went through and their emotional support, I also thank my writers group fellows from River City Ink: Stephanie Daily, Joy Elkins, Frank Kavanaugh, Alexandra Marbach, Barbara O'Connor, Manuela Stafford; and the New Braunfels Writers Guild: Betty Cook, Hollis Danvers, Donna Heath, Anna Manning, Don Manusos, Peter Olsen and Lewis Sarkozi.

Vince Linger, my "little brother," took the cover photo of Mittens and me (in a blonder moment.) My life-long buddy Glen Fulce, took the picture of me on the back. Thank you guys. You always make me look good.

September is National Suicide Prevention Month. Check your local area for emergency phone numbers and organizations that provide prevention and crisis intervention services.

Naomi Patterson

Death By Catgut

Contents

Death By Catgut

Cat and Mouse

I didn't start my life wanting to be known as the town's "senile soothsayer." I wanted to be an astronaut zoologist. My reputation as the witchy-woman who whispered other people's futures to them from the back table at Claire's Bar and Grill grew gradually, jigger by jigger. I tried sobriety, once, for a month. I couldn't face my clients' dreams and disappointments with the "clean and sober" token from Alcoholics Anonymous in my pocket and no vodka in my system. So, I tossed my AA keepsake and picked up my granny's deck of Tarot cards to embrace my family's psychic heritage. I became Angel Falls' version of the *Twin Peaks* Log Lady, the "tipsy teller of tall tales" who lived at Seven Hilltop Street with cats. Lots of cats.

In my dreams, I lived in a Thomas Kinkade cottage surrounded by forest and an English flower garden. My open-eyed home was a dilapidated, two and a half-story fish

1

mercantile building that had been abandoned, foreclosed, and auctioned off. I bought the old building with delusions of distressed deconstructionism. Harvey, my best friend moved in with me. He added to the escrow with muscle-money to make the place livable. I *thought* I wanted a teahouse; Harvey, an art studio. I *felt* if I surrounded myself with enough Earl Grey, doilies, and lace napkins I could survive my own deconstructionism.

Harv and I buried our entrepreneur goals, along with a few other things, but did enough renovation on the outside of the house to keep from getting any yellow "do not cross" tape on the front doors. Inside, we made do with hand-me-down furniture, junkyard windowpanes, and rummage sale castaways. Our needs weren't great, except for kitty kibbles. The creek around us dried up long before we bought the place. We shared our "closed" cannery with seventeen cats, a polar bear rug, a giraffe coat rack, an elephant-foot footstool, and all manner of critters from Noah's Ark displayed in still-life splendor.

Harvey practiced the art and skill of taxidermy. His talent involved skill because it took detailed knowledge of animal anatomy to rebuild a beasty correctly, and art because it was difficult to keep said reconstructions looking pretty. I named the creatures that passed through my housemate's third floor workshop. It helped me get over the "yew, that's a dead, stuffed animal" aspects of Harv's hobby. However, I stopped giving the deer heads monikers after I ran through Santa's sleigh-pulling friends the fourth time around.

How did I end up living like this?

My mother asked me similar questions in her final years. How did this happen? How did you turn into this? The "this" she spoke of was never specifically identified, but in mother-daughter vernacular, "this" meant not what she expected or wanted.

"You are not my daughter. You belong to your father, hook, line and sinker." Her words echoed in my mind beyond her living years. I was the daughter of her body, but not her heart. I tried to please Mom, but more times than not I proved to be a disappointment. Every child brings her mother wildflowers, but my bouquet contained ragweed. To her credit, she put my gift in a vase on the table. The whole family sneezed for a week. My three older brothers fared better in Mama's judgment. In her estimation, I lacked some necessary equipment to succeed: a husband to tell me what to do, or "XY" genitalia. I was, therefore, limited. Her assessment of me was not intentionally cruel. She lived and thought as a product of her time.

A mini-miscreant can only blame her family of origin for

3

so long before it changes from a reason for odd behavior to a lame excuse.

My father, Benjamin, enjoyed the Army way of life. My mother, Gina, strove to be the picture perfect image of a military wife. Dad was the Officer on Duty: Mom, the Company Commander. As children our lives were structured, ordered, disciplined. Raising three boys came naturally to them. They didn't know what to do with a girl. The men in my family doted on and revered my mother. She reigned as queen bee until I came along late in their lives.

I was a challenging toddler, a difficult teenager, and an interesting young adult.

Interesting being akin to the Chinese curse: "May you live an interesting life."

It didn't help that I was an unattractive child. My mother pin-curled or home-permed my hair as best she could. However, two minutes after she finished any style, I looked disheveled. Much to my mother's chagrin, her little girl's idea of dress-up included a pair of big brothers' faded jeans and a tee shirt rather than lace and rhinestones. I think Mama wanted a princess to follow her to the family throne. Unfortunately for both of us, she got a tomboy who suffered from chemically abused hair and skinned knees. At the age of twelve, I shaved my head in protest and refused to wear anything with flowers on it.

So, that was that.

I inherited my dad's "headaches," as he called them, and his penchant for self-medication. My Dad called his medicinal preference Seven-N-Seven-N-Seven. He claimed in seven minutes Seagram's Seven and Seven-Up would relieve his pain.

"Cube me a seven, darling. I don't want to see what happens next," his long dead voice whispered in my mind.

Sometimes his remedy worked for me and blurred the images. Sometimes they came anyway and the cure could be worse that the cause. Daddy thought his visions meant he was crazy. Mama thought so too. I wished that I could have told them different. Daddy knew things, lots of things, as they happened and before they happened. His mother, my Granny Winnie, did too.

Born Winifred Dorkus Cude, Granny was a black-headed firecracker. She stayed with us whenever Daddy's duty station placed us close enough for her to visit. Her favorite tee shirt read, "I am the crazy grandmother the rest of the family warned you about." She taught me how to hunt for dragons in flower gardens and how to listen for their singing. I loved my Granny Winnie. She was half-breed Comanche and proud of it.

Daddy's birthright made him an American Indian

quadroon with beautiful copper skin, black hair, and chocolate eyes. Outsourcing genetics through marriage graced my brothers, two of our close cousins, and me with the ability to tan without burning, and one-eighth possibility of shaman abilities. A blood infusion from the Scottish highlands gave the six of us reddish brown hair and blue-green eyes.

In their last days, my parents became mirror images. Through her Alzheimer's haze, Mom didn't remember what happened in the morning, but she was keen on what took place thirty years ago. Ben and Gina balanced each other out: one looked into the future and one looked into the past. I had the ability to look in both directions.

Can't say as I like the view either way.

Hiding from the world on our sectional sofa seemed like a good idea this morning. Harvey and I jokingly referred to this area of the house as the second floor media room. Here we displayed one 12 inch black and white TV. It's not that we wouldn't have appreciated a new 42 inch flat screen, but we needed cat food more. We continued our shabby chic decor with an emergency hand crank flashlight, a ham radio set with frayed wires, and a kerosene lamp as "found art" homage to the movie *Independence Day*. We kept a Morse Code telegraph apparatus mixed in with our books and other nick-knacks on the built in bookcases, along side a broken IBM Selectric typewriter with the "a" and "l" keys missing. There were several carcasses of off-brand computers that completed our self-labeled "lack of technology" display.

Our handmade wooden entertainment center sported an honest-to-God record player and twenty-five surviving LPs. We had books stacked everywhere. A tick-tock cat clock hung on the wall with the pendulum tail and moving eyeballs, along with two hideously mounted singing fish.

Cause, you know, one big-mouth Bass belting out "Joy to the World" is just not enough.

Three cat condominiums with scratching posts grew into the Kitty-A-Go-Go party platform that ran the circumference of the great room. The cat platforms attached to one another via rope bridges, hammocks, and walkways that Harvey and I built out of old rope and scrap lumber. This construction allowed our cats to cross the room without touching the floor. A cat-shaped, catnip piñata hanging in the corner completed our kitty retreat.

The loft had been office space on the second floor of the fish building that collapsed into a symmetrical pattern after the explosion of '97.

Not my fault. I didn't even live here then. I think it had something to do with a case of homemade beer hidden in one of the closets.

No support walls were damaged by the mini-kaboom, and the area actually looked planned. We'd contracted necessary workers to repair the sub-flooring and railing, but we did the mud-tape-float ourselves. The mezzanine-style open formant worked, but wanted paint. We also needed to do roof repairs or the next Poseidon and Thor tantrum might wash us away from the inside out.

Yes, I mix mythologies. I mix a lot of things. However, I prefer mixing Crown Royal and Diet Coke.

Harvey appeared in front of me by the sofa with a trash bag in his hands. "Will you switch from whiskey back to wine, or better, beer?" Harvey dumped two empty Jim Beam bottles into the Friday trash. "You have to work tonight, and you'll scare off customers with your breath."

I shuffled the dragon-marked Tarot cards I held in my hands, and narrowed my eyes to stare at him. I tossed down a Seven-Card Choice Spread on top of our exotic driftwood and glass coffee table. Harvey's Auntie Barbara gave us the table as a house-warming gift. When she made the table, she hid twinkle lights in the twisted folds of wood. On top sat a wavy sea-blue glass that mesmerized anyone who looked through it at night. A silent sea with stars reflected in unmoving waves.

Death By Catgut

Auntie Barb traveled the world as a Talent Manager. Her ability to produce needed "riders" to contracts for celebrities aided her success. As teenagers, Harvey and I helped her pick the green M & Ms out of several bags so the rock star she chaperoned could have his bowl of "green only" candies. We got backstage passes for our efforts. Barbara was in her own right a recognized artist, musician, antiquities dealer, and quite possibly a tomb raider.

The fact that she makes me appear sane is at once comforting and scary.

I put an air fern and seashells atop the ocean glass. For me the table held the elements: the twinkle lights as Fire, the seashells as Water, the wood as Earth, the plant as Air, and Auntie Barb's art and effort as Spirit. Today it also held an empty pizza box I pushed in Harvey's direction to make room for my cards.

I flipped over the first Tarot card. That position referred to an event in Life (Option A). Dragon Lovers embraced facing upside down. Upside down meant a negative romantic encounter. Harvey and I were not paramours; he was more like a fourth brother. I had a damn good idea whom the cards meant.

It's a special time of year for me.

Card number two suggested a course of action. The third

card pronounced the outcome if Option A was chosen. I used this particular design for myself because there was a get-out-of-jail-free plan, known as Option B. Card four pointed to the predicaments associated with said plan B. I drew The Hermit.

Great! Just what I need: more solitude.

I kept cards five and six facing down and flipped over the card that suggested my best course of action. The Magician took on a sinister aspect in the upside down position. It indicated an encounter with a con artist, being surrounded by liars, and far-reaching deceptions.

Crap, crap, crap. Reshuffling the deck is cheating.

Maybe if I left them on the table one of the cats would rearrange them for me. They regularly changed my perspective. Cats understood all things as transitory. Their metaphysical abilities allowed them to view frowns as merely smiles waiting for a turnaround.

Harvey cleared his throat. Lost in my own thoughts, I had momentarily forgotten he stood there. I belched and sank into the sectional where three of our kitties and I had made a nest with pillows and lap robes. I offered up two empty Sam Adams bottles from beneath the sofa cushions for Harvey. He stared into the dark corner of the loft, holding the black plastic garbage bag in his hands like a shield. He shuddered.

I sat up and looked over the back of the couch. "What are you seeing?"

"Nothing," he mumbled.

"You got the whim-whams?"

"Sure, sure . . . the whim-whams," he answered, but his eyes were unfocused.

Harvey can't deal with his ability to touch the unknown. My housemate calls messages he gets from the beyond a hunch and leaves the veil crossings to me.

Perhaps my father's inability to deal with what he saw on the other side of reality was why he left to check out the darkness on his own terms. I didn't understand when Daddy gave my brothers and me the "Face Your Fears" speech that it included death, his death and more specifically him killing himself. I'm from the generation of women who grew up believing that men didn't leave their families.

Go to war, yes, but off to contemplate the meaning of life, the purpose of navel lint, or suicide not expectable.

"Come on, Maximus Catus," Harvey hollered. "There's trash to be collected, lizards to be chased."

"Mip," Max answered.

Max, our eighteen-pound chocolate Siamese, oversaw all outside activities. For being such a huge beastie, he had a sissy voice that came out like a whispered chirp. His glacier-blue eyes reminded me of my mother's.

"Wait. I found one more," I said pulling an empty Budweiser can out of my shoe.

Harvey tussled with the trash bag while I finished searching my surroundings for more hidden treasures. Toby, our one-eyed Tabby head-butted and scent marked Harv's shins with his whisker musk, while they waited on me. Harvey was the alpha male in our cat colony. My own position was nebulas. I was no longer the alpha female. Twilight claimed that title, but I was the great food provider. As such I garnered affection, if not respect.

"Thanks, buddy," Harvey said, tugging on the Tabby's tail. "You want to come with us to the dumpster? We'll make it an adventure."

"You asked me to go back to drinking beer and/or wine. Why? What does it matter what I drink?"

"Because," Harvey's voice was low, "you're not mean when you drink wine, more whimsical. Hard liquor makes you hard."

"And beer?" I found his observation curious.

"You become sleepy. I know you're trying to cut down on our trips to the ER for pain meds, but I can tell the difference between a migraine and a hangover. You're killing yourself."

I pretended he shot an arrow into my heart, then pulled it out and moved it to my head. "What's another ghost in the house?"

"One too many."

Naomi Patterson

Visitors at the Asylum

Harvey and I were childhood friends. As elementary kids, we were small and scrawny for our age. In middle school, we figured out if we fought the bullies back to back we lasted longer. Not necessarily a good thing, it prolonged our misery. Eventually, one of us went down or wet our pants. We never felt the need to point out our failures to one another, which made his attitude this morning seem out of place.

As boys often do, he sprouted tall the summer after high school into a slender, nicely muscled six-foot, three inches. Me, not so much; I stayed a foot under him. Harvey went off to college. I could have gone too, but I opted out of higher education for a chance to work the graveyard shift at the twenty-four hour Wal-Mart. Mom's melancholy had changed into the first stage of Alzheimer's. I didn't have a clue what was going on, only that Mama acted a bit spacey and I needed to stay near her. Working nights while she slept gave me days to be with her.

I raise my empty beer bottle to the paths not taken.

I had multiple odd jobs, after that, but settled in as a receptionist for our local veterinary office. A decade ago I also began moonlighting at Claire's Bar and Grill as a psychic when Judy, her regular soothsayer, needed the night off. Harvey dropped out of his pre-med program because of money issues and got a job at the H.E.B. He was a highly respected manager who tried to keep his private life private, while living with one of the town criers. Not an easy task. The fact that he had been stuffing animals, as a hobby, since he was twelve wasn't talked about in mixed company unless the conversation shifted to serial killers in training.

Teasing, just teasing.

Harv viewed the physiology of any reconstruction subject as a puzzle. He took no pleasure in death. Nor did I.

Horror movies not withstanding, the process of passing away was more often than not a peaceful release. At the vet clinic, Dr. Word made the technical aspects of the end of life gentle, emotionally and physically, on both pets and their humans. We did in-home euthanasia, when we could, so the animals stayed in familiar surrounding. When that was not possible, we asked the family to provide a towel, a tee shirt, a sock, a favorite toy . . . something that smelled like home to comfort the animal.

I hadn't gone through the tech classes, so I was not legally allowed to insert an IV, but I had a soothing voice, calm touch, and the temperament to hold dying pets during their last moments, if their humans could only watch and cry. Most animals liked having me around.

As to the mechanics of death, Dr. Word inserted the IV out of an owner's sight, but the final injections were done in the arms of a loved one. I respected Dr. Word. She did all that she could as a healer, and then did what she had to. She used the two shot method for euthanasia. First, she gave the patient a sedative to relax. Often as the pain eased in the animal, stress also lessoned in their human.

I believe a whispered "I love you" can be heard in those final moments. I have to.

After the last hugs were given, Dr. Word discretely administered the second drug, a barbiturate that stopped the heart. In seconds a loving companion went boneless, breathless, and beyond any torment of this world.

I wish the same kindness for humans.

Harvey and I both dealt with death on a regular basis. It was one of our binding threads. We weren't made of the same cloth, but we were definitely woven on the same loom. Unofficial housemates off and on since college, we slept on each other's sofa in between apartments and lovers, and became official co-homeowners when I bought the house on Hilltop. He grew up with two sisters and intuitively knew which week of the month to throw a box of chocolate in my bedroom and run; however, recognizing when my "headaches" started had more to do with him than me. Harvey was extremely observant and detail-oriented.

"How do you know when my head is ready to explode?"

"When you get a migraine your eyes go to soft focus. You talk slow, like you have to translate the words from another language, working out the pronunciation; and you become snarky around loud noises and bright lights."

"'Snarky?' Been reading my Janet Evanovich novels?"

"It's a good word," he admitted, "And you do remind me of Stephanie's Grandma Mazur."

I had nothing left to throw at him, but he was probably correct. "It's too early for this kind of attitude from you. What's wrong, a monkey's paw gone missing from your la-bor-a-tory? You misplace a mousetrap or some catgut?"

"You're the one who collects odd artifacts. You and my Auntie."

Harvey haphazardly pointed to my "collectables" spaced throughout the bookshelves where cat tails were less likely to knock them off shelves. My eyes traced his movement. If I were an estate salesperson, my heart would leap for joy at the ceramic faeries, stuffed dragons, miniature castles and crystals that lay about.

Then again, maybe not. Post Modernism Fey décor doesn't appeal to everyone.

Harv clinked empty Samuel Adams Merry Mischief bottles together. "I see you need another beer. By the way, this is the good stuff. I hid a case, but we won't get this again until next winter. The brewery has moved on to their spring collection. Don't waste this by letting it go flat or giving it to the cats."

Tux, one of our black and white cats, liked beer. He bit my toes if I didn't give him a sip of Samuel. Harvey knew that. I didn't understand what bugged my roomie this morning. Friday was my day off, until the evening shift at Claire's Bar and Grill. Heavy emphasis on bar. Harvey normally didn't care how I spent my mornings.

"If you're going to be pissy, I'm going to ignore you." I went back to my cards and flipped over the second position.

"Stop it. You don't get to read me, Nan." He scattered

the cards and the cats.

"Hey," I shouted. "That's not your future you dumped on the floor. Geeze! You *need* a girlfriend."

"I *need* a sober housemate," he chided.

"More than you *need* a free place to live?"

Harvey set his jaw and rubbed his tongue over his teeth with a loud smack. That gesture was one of his anger "tells." He did it to keep himself from saying something mean. What I said wasn't fair, and I was sorry the minute it came out of my mouth. My inheritance paid for the fish house, but Harvey's labors made it habitable. Sweat equity counted.

"I pay my share." He huffed. "I didn't sign up for a lifetime of being your bodyguard. I'm not up for this shit, again."

"Not up for what?" I asked.

Most of the time I kept up with Harv when he jumped conversational tracks, but this morning he wheeled to nowhere. I hiccupped. It became a verp. Punkin turned her tail to me when she smelled my breath. I made my scrunchie face.

"You're not going to puke are you?" Harvey offered me the empty pizza box to barf in.

I gave him the thumbs-up hand sign, folded back into the mid-section of the sedative sofa, and grabbed Punkin back into my arms as a safety blanket.

Punkin was one of the five orange colored kitties we fed, housed, and would send to college, if someone opened a feline university. Solid orange female cats were rare, as were calico males. She was smart, funny, and an easy purr. Her biological heritage came from a Maine Coon line mixed with wild alley rat chaser. Punkin loved to be with me in our garden where she napped under the broccoli, while I weeded and planted new seeds. She had soft, silky long hair rather than fur, and she snuggled with me even under the worst of conditions. When the pounding, puking, "shoot me" part of a migraine hit me, it was Punkin who sat in the bathroom beside me. She had an empathetic soul, and touching her made me feel better. I would never tell Harvey, but Punkin was my favorite.

It's not fair to put one child above the others, two- or four-footed, but it happens.

"Don't suffocate my cat," demanded Harvey.

He watched Punkin and me as we became one with the sofa.

"Punkin's not yours, she's ours."

"I found her, she's mine."

"You gave her to me. Besides who's sleeping on whose boobs?" I asked, and pointed at the soft tuft of orange fluff content to sleep across my chest until I burped again.

Harvey laughed in spite of himself. "That's unfair. I am genetically designed for harder muscles than you. You are cheating, using feminine wiles and softness against me. You have seventeen other cats to torment, you know."

"Not all of them are warm."

I nodded toward Stanley, the stuffed saber-toothed Ragdoll that eternally guarded the unused hallway to our unused guest bedrooms. A forgotten friend, in dental school at the time, created longer canine teeth that Harvey affixed to the cat. Ragdolls were one of the biggest breeds of domestic cat to begin with, and Stanley measured in on the tall end of show cat standards.

"Fifteen living cats," he admitted. "But, don't discount ol' Stan. He's a pip, even dead."

Pip? Harvey's watching way too much BBC America on the black and white telly.

Stanley found me the afternoon of my dad's closed-casket funeral. Statistics showed women didn't want to mess up their faces when they killed themselves, but men had no compunction about sticking a shotgun in their mouths, or putting a revolver to the temple and blowing off half their heads. Daddy had the decency to shoot himself behind the shed, so we didn't have to see the Technicolor evidence of our loss every time we came home. What the coroner didn't pick up got eaten by critters and washed away with the rain that came two days later. Or maybe it was one of my big brothers and the water hose . . . life's little mysteries.

Stanley came to me deeply in need of TLC. I discovered him in the graveyard trying to hide behind Mrs. Iona Stanley's tombstone, hence his name. Bone-thin after I shaved his matted fur, he was three and a half feet nose to tip of tail. By the time I finished with him he weighed in at twenty pounds. Stanley didn't live long, but his last years were surrounded in food, warmth, loving touches, and unconditional acceptance.

Not bad as the end to a life goes. I've seen worse.

In due course, Stanley's reconstructed form kept company with four raccoons, Eenie, Meenie, Meinie, Moe; a full-bodied baby moose, Bullwinkle; a two headed lamb, Gads-Zooks, who'd been discarded from a traveling circus; a polar bear rug, Snowflake (another gift from Auntie Barb); and an old mountain lion, Sienna, who died in her sleep at our small, now defunct local zoo.

Harvey and I helped with the necropsy on the big cat and were given the remains to dispose of as we saw fit. Eventually, Sienna would end up in a museum or one of the Cabela's dioramas along with all our guests, but for now they were part of the family. Various other critters from the bird and reptile species stayed on the third floor where no leaks came through the shingles, but I didn't allow the reptile gods downstairs with the rest of us.

A girl has to set some limits. God knows my boundaries are blurry enough as it is.

We had inherited a number of large specimens from Auntie Barbara. To be honest, the collection grossed me out. Not from the emotional atrocity of killing such magnificent creatures, although it should. Most of our exotic friends had been dead for more than a half a century, and the pain from their passing had faded from tangible energy fields long ago. It was Jumba's toenails that disturbed me. The elephant's toenails were too long, a greyish-yellow, in want of a trim and dusting. One of Giselle's glass eyes sat crooked in the socket, and the poor pelican looked to be in mid-molt. I occasionally stood amongst the assortment imagining my own post-mortem preservation.

Look closely, folks, at this umbrella stand. Here we find a rare specimen of crazyus-womanity, recycled-repurposed.

Punkin stretched into wakefulness and jumped down. I was not inclined to join her. Harvey brought me a third beer as an apology for his outburst, and left me to my soft breakfast buzz. He had morning chores: discarding a week's worth of frozen dinner containers, emptying litter box excrements, and dragging the trash bin to the big dumpster at the corner of our lot. He'd finish by mopping the kitchen. One day, we'd have to do something with all our unused space . . . a parlor, an office, a library and dining room, perhaps that small art gallery with a couple of tables for tea.

I'd get to the dusting and laundry later. Besides, Harvey was right: I had to work my corner at Claire's Bar and Grill tonight. I needed to put enough liquid "medication" in me to get through all my clients' hopes and dreams. Broken or realized their wishes drained energy from me if I didn't protect myself. No matter how many times I lay down to sleep with Samuel, Jose, or Jack, I always woke up alone, and did what I did the day before: the human version of running on a hamster wheel, my version of *Groundhog's Day.*

Through the open windows I heard Harvey walking down our driveway and recognized Max's chirrup as he padded after the big man, admonishing Harv to wait for him.

Our address was a partial misnomer. We did have a wooded area behind us that sort of looked like a small hill and from the third floor we could see into the town, but the "Hilltop" nickname got started because the house sat on stilts in an empty creek area the long-forgotten fish company created to dump the guts of their daily catch down a chute and into the water. With the aid of a water wheel the unused fish parts were returned to one of the two rivers that ran through town. A dam closed down the business, and took care of the backwash. Our cats liked the leftover ambiance, so the old water wheel turned into a planter.

Although we huddled on the ground floor in the winter months, as the first whispers of spring blew in, man, woman and beasties scattered to our various floors. Harvey and any projects he was working on bolted for the third level. Most of the cats homesteaded the second floor, me with them. From the outside, our unusual family and living situation suggested Harvey and I were antisocial. That wasn't true. We simply preferred the company of animals to that of most humans.

Harvey and I also shared a macabre curiosity about death. I think it started when we were in seventh grade and found a mouse in my Mom's pantry, trapped but not yet dead. The mousetrap was designed to snap the creature's neck in a humane demise.

Trust me on this one, not humane.

My mother screeched as she entered the kitchen and saw the mouse writhing in pain. "Get that thing out of here!" she shouted, as she puffed on an unfiltered Camel cigarette.

Harv and I carried it to the backyard. The wounded mouse was beyond healing. Even as children, we understood pain, fear, and compassion. I'm not sure where Harvey found the courage, but he reached under the mouse's chin and, as tenderly as he could, finished breaking its neck. From that point on, he knew how easy it was to end a life . . . and so did I.

Death By Catgut

The Crown and a Fool

My long-standing obligation to show up at Claire's Bar and Grill on Friday nights and tell fortunes started out as a joke. I dressed as a witch for one Halloween and offered to give Judy, Angel Fall's real Psychic in Residence, the night off. I flew in on my broomstick, pulled out a pack of Tarot cards, and an Angel Falls tradition was born.

My weekly appearance had been a spot of contention between my lover and me, when he lived. It wasn't because I spent four nights a month in a bar, but that I actually believed the fortunes I told. Doc told me I was a fool to have faith in such gobbledygook. I didn't bother to point out that at certain times in our human history his precious science appeared to be supernatural nonsense. No room for magic or magick in his life.

Magic being a performance art, and magick being the Craft connotation for the ability to bring about change through

Naomi Patterson

extraordinary means.

I didn't need the Tarot cards to do what I did, but they gave my clients something to focus on, and my hands something to fidget with as I translated wisdom from the "Powers That Be" to the questioner in need.

The deck I used came to me as a gift from my Granny Winifred. She taught me how to read the Three-Card Method and the Simple Cross Spread when I was a child. I favored them when I divined for the general public. My deck had one grand dragon on the back and different dragon characters on the face side. The deck felt comfortable in my hands with its worn edges and bent corners. When I asked Granny Winnie how she knew what the cards were saying, her answer was, "The dragons sing to me."

My observations, akin to my grandmother's, came from a different, less tangible emotional and spiritual level that she and I could sometimes tap into. That ability, with a dash of common sense, an understanding of human nature, and the old fashioned notion of listening more than I spoke, made me one of the two renowned psychics in town.

Go figure.

Granny told me my Raven Spirit Guide would answer my questions and lead me through the pathways on the other side. The Indian part of my grandmother believed in spirit guides, dream catchers, and medicine wheels. I thought they were cool, before I understood how precarious walking the other side could be, or the truth in Edgar Allen Poe's writing.

I would prefer to commune with a monkey, a lemur – hello, a cat perhaps or even a pot-bellied pig – before a sarcastic, hoppy blackbird with an attitude, but I didn't get a vote.

My fortune-telling mien had a sinister appeal that I enjoyed playing. I wasn't Goth, not really. My body wasn't covered in tattoos that sagged with age, inappropriate piercings, or ownership brands. I happened to look good in dark colors, and you can hide a multitude of sin, as well as the effects of too many Crown Royal shots, in black, dark purple, and midnight blue.

Sometimes Mittens and Marmalade accompanied me to the Bar and Grill. They were twin Maine Coon cats who liked the attention and snacks they got when they came along. Claire's dog, Mutt, enjoyed their companionship. Mittens often joined in on a card reading. He jumped into my lap to paw at the cards. My regulars enjoyed his participation. I told new clients that he had the power to change their fortunes. When my cat batted at a card in a negative position, I flipped it into a positive one.

Everyone needs a bit of cat luck. Ask Maneki Neko, the Japanese waving cat that appears in Asian restaurants.

On a good night, at thirty-five dollars a pop, I could clear hundred dollars at the B & G. Even a slow night with only whining teenagers to see, I brought home enough cash to buy more kibbles. I hoped this would be a full night of reads.

The problem with drinking beer for breakfast was that the buzz didn't last. By noon the hops had faded. I was wide-awake and pissed at the world for no particular reason. My beer-drinking buddy, Tux, head-butted me, and lifted my chin toward the bug-eyed cat clock. There was time enough for me to tinker in my herb garden before I got dressed in my witch costume for Claire's.

"Garden!" I yelled.

Five feline herbalists manifested at my side. Down the stairs, we pussyfooted through the kitchen to the back courtyard, with Punkin in the lead. Sometimes her tail came in tinted green from being wrapped around plants. Cricket and Sammie tussled for a dead lizard. Toby and Phizner went off to chase butterflies.

I pulled an early blooming dandelion out of the soft soil roots and all. Sure, they're intruders in a well-groomed garden, but I liked the dots of yellow color. They brightened even gloomy days and moods. I had fond memories of blowing wishes into the wind with Granny when the yellow weeds turned into puffs of white. I teased Punkin with the flower in my hand. She took the bait and quickly ripped it to pieces. No playing "he love me-he loves me not" with the petals for her.

Smart girl.

Today, I felt the need for rosemary. Shakespeare said it was for remembrance, but in herbal folklore it also had properties of protection. I tied small nosegays with pieces of rosemary, lavender, and mint. In a more romantic time, each flower symbolized an emotion or carried a secret meaning, a pretty but limited vernacular.

The tips of my yellow daffodils were poking their heads up. Doc gave me daffodils. As one of the first flowers of spring, they represented rebirth and new beginnings, faithfulness, and honesty. Supposedly, they returned even after the harshest of winters and deepest of sorrows.

Too bad herbs didn't help me. Five milligrams of Valium with a Crown Royal chaser worked better in my system. Nonetheless, I stuck a sprig of rosemary behind my ear.

A couple of the nearby restaurants bought my aromatic plants in season. Claire sold dried packets of my herbs, strictly non-medicinal, in the tchotchke corner of her establishment. I made her keep the money to balance out the bar tab I never seemed to receive.

Everything in the garden needed watering. I did my rain dance. It wasn't pretty. I looked like I was trying to do the Hokey-Pokey, the Macarena, and the Jerk all at the same time. I waited a minute, danced a little more, then gave in and turned the sprinkler on. I nipped and snipped here and there, but it was early in the season. Merlin, one of our solid black cats, dug a hole by the parsley. He was not planting seeds. There was enough time for a nap before the evening's events.

"Inside!" I called.

All the felines who wanted back in followed at my heels.

#

I got to Claire's early. I swirled through the front door and posed by her fake fichus tree, for which I received a small round of applause. Using my cape, I flapped over to "my" barstool. I sported a conical hat and a black wig. To finish the witch effect, I wore lots of black eyeliner, long eyelashes and painted fingernails in oxblood red with a matching shade of lipstick. Whether I looked cool or scary in my outfit depended on how many drinks I'd had.

Claire was my buddy. I guess, my only other human friend besides Harvey and Judy. The lady barkeep had a double shot of Crown Royal waiting for me. My conversation with Harvey from this morning came back to me. I'd switch to beer later. There was no need to be mean spirited this early in the night.

Part of her bar had been built out of an old teak sailboat. Rumors were that Claire had sailed that boat around the world by herself in her younger years. She'd been chased by modern day pirates in the Caribbean, tipped sideways in the Pacific by migrating humpback whales, and almost frozen to death in the Baltic Sea.

Here in Angel Falls, she dropped anchor. I'm not sure if she got tired of pirates, decided she didn't like the taste of salt water, or got bored with traveling. Life happened and sometimes folks got weary of their wandering ways. She was small, like me, but with highlighted-blond hair and smile lines on her sun-tanned face.

We clinked shot glasses.

"To the worst of 'em gone before us," Claire spoke our traditional Friday night greeting.

I never knew if she referred to men or days. I answered, "And to the best of 'em yet to come."

She had a pottery jar on the bar inscribed "The Ashes of Past Lovers." Whenever a handsome tourist came into the Bar and Grill, his first drink was on the house. She would gesture to the jar as she brought his choice of poison and say, "You can't be first, honey, but you can be next." Claire always received a smile and sometimes a large tip.

We knocked the Crowns back, and I headed for my table. The white butcher paper square on top, a token homage to tablecloths, was smooth enough for me to spread out the tools of my trade. Some showmanship was expected when I performed at the B & G. I lit a couple of candles, prominently displayed my crystal ball, and placed some cute ceramic dragons on the table. There was a small nautical flag in the center with salt and pepper shakers in the shape of lighthouses, which I pushed to the side.

The sole barmaid, Claire's niece Laura, brought me a glass of water with a second shot of Crown as I took out my herbal bundles and laid them around the table. I offered her a nosegay. She curtsied and placed it in her blouse pocket. A sprig of lavender peeked up over the edge.

"Don't let that fall into someone's dinner," I teased her.

"If Aunt Claire is cooking tonight, it can only help." Laura laughed and winked at me.

"Where's JD?"

Laura shrugged and went back to polishing glasses at the

bar.

I arranged my tabletop, surrounding myself with representations of the four elements: fire, water, earth and air. I provided the fifth aspect of spirit. I described myself as a Wiccan/Christian or a Druid with a carpenter addiction. More than an ambivalent agnostic, I enjoyed the idea of a savior but wouldn't change my ability to touch our metaphysical world. In the eyes of the Fundamentalists, I was a heretic. If God created angels and demons, then I believed he/she/they could also have made faeries and dragons. *Fool though I may be, with or without the help of Crown, my body sways to the rhythms of old-world wisdoms.* Lucky for me, the lumber mill shut down in Angel Falls a long time ago.

My special-needs client stood quietly by the next table with curly fries in one hand and his tattered Mobil baseball cap in the other. The cap was so old it had the ARCO red horse with wings as the logo. Jimmy never went anywhere without it. He suffered with Adult Attention Deficit Disorder and had trouble being still for any length of time. He always came in thirty minutes before he figured I'd be there, ordered some food to play with, then waited, as patiently as he could, until I invited him to sit down.

Jimmy was one of my regulars who worked at, and in

fact owned, the town's only gas station. I charged him ten dollars a session. It's not that he couldn't afford more, but he rarely sat with me long enough for a full reading. I think some weeks I was his single point of human contact, outside of a "Thank you, Sir," or "Here is your change, Ma'am." Besides, I'm a sucker for big honey amber eyes in men or cats.

"Hey Jimmy, why don't you take a seat?" I invited.

"Mind if I bring my curly fries, Miss Nan?"

"Not if you share."

He sat. I shuffled the cards, reached for a couple of spicy curls and washed them down with my complimentary drink. There was an art if not a skill to my cartomancy. I adjusted my layout to the needs of my clients and/or last call at the bar. I kept away from using the full deck of seventy-eight cards, preferring to use only the twenty-two Major Arcana in a Weekly-Forecast design.

Jimmy enjoyed the big twelve-card Horoscope Spread. He liked seeing all those dragons displayed on my table. The first card represented the personality of the questioner. As part of our fun, each Friday we tried to guess who he was this week: the fool, a lover, the sage, or a king.

"How's it going, Jimmy?" I asked.

"Same ol' -- same ol'," he answered with a mouth full of

potatoes.

I took his greasy fingers in my hands, and squeezed them as an affectionate greeting (and to get as much grease off as I could before he started poking at my cards). As I held his hand a shiver went through me. Jimmy looked the same, but he felt different, kind of hollow. I pushed a rosemary-mint-lavender posy in his direction. He inhaled the fragrant mixture. He seemed to relax, but it was difficult to tell with him.

Jimmy pointed to the first card, and offered me more fries. "I put jalapeno flavored sea salt on them. So, who am I tonight?"

"Thanks," I said taking one more fry. I lifted the edge of the first card so only I could see it to tease him.

The Death Dragon. I got a sharp stabbing pain in my left temple. The Death Dragon stared back at me from his empty skeletal sockets, right side up and in full threat mode. The scythe-wielding wyvern heralded death, but it also symbolized the end of an era, a changed attitude. It could mean the conclusion of a business relationship or termination of a love affair. It didn't have to mean dead-dead.

The music on the jukebox clattered between my ears. The light around Jimmy went blurry. His whole body washed in a blue haze. He looked like an angel with his blond hair forming a soft, golden halo around his sweet face. I felt the beginning of my fall, but not the end.

Crap, crap, crap.

Death By Catgut

Ordinary Daze

I'm not sure how long I lay unconscious on the floor. When I opened my eyes, Claire stood over me waving a chili-stained bar towel at me. The leftover aroma did nothing for my queasy stomach. I lay on my back in a most immodest sprawl. My black wig sat cocked sideways on my head, and my hat was next to my feet. I pulled my faux locks off, letting loose my own waist-length, reddish-brownish-greyish hair. I grabbed my pointy hat, and plopped it back on my head as I sat up. Jimmy's curly fries were all gone.

Wow, must have been out for a long time.

Jimmy whispered, "Pretty hair, Miss Nan."

"Thanks," I slurred and left it at that. I was not into the whole "cougar crush" phenomena.

Not unless pretty-boy actors Nathan Fillion or Timothy Olyphant suddenly become interested in an unknown, middle-

aged, veterinarian's assistant.

Besides, to play in that arena you needed to be rich and/or powerful and/or beautiful. I was more a dark version of a Raggedy Ann doll shaken upside down until her pigtails unraveled, not an eccentric collector of young men. Even so, the sweetness of Jimmy's compliment made my head hurt less. Not much, but less. The universe lunged again and my mind went with it.

"Sweetness," a long lost voice whispered in my ear.

I smelled daffodils. Not an easy scent to define. I searched the room for Doc, and there he stood behind Jimmy. I reached for him, but he didn't move. His hazel eyes closed, and I watched a single tear run down his pale cheek.

"Come home," I mumbled. I realized everyone was staring at me, and I put my arms down.

Claire pulled my face toward her. She looked back over her, but Doc was already gone. She took my hat back off and handed it to Jimmy.

I felt like a bobble-head toy. "What?" I wiped a bit of drool from the edge of my mouth.

"Focus, on me," she demanded. "Eyes on me, girlfriend. No, no, Nan, both of them. Come on, look this way."

She moved her index finger back and forth in front of

me. I seriously considered grabbing her hand. She was making me seasick.

"Why's everyone staring at me?" I asked.

"Oh, no reason," snorted Laura over Claire's shoulder.

After a minute more, I could focus. I didn't understand why, but when I had one of my *spells,* it was difficult to look straight into someone's eyes. Once I managed orb-to-orb contact, everyone knew I was over the worst part.

"That's more like it." Claire sounded relieved. "She's back. Help me get her on the chair, Jimmy. Better make it a chair with arms."

Jimmy's man-child touch was apprehensive. He didn't know what part of my body would be appropriate to take hold of. He took a deep breath, grabbed me around the middle from behind, like a three-year old picks up a big fat cat, and lifted me onto an armchair. His strength surprised me. His height and build made him a little guy, in my mind, about five-foot six inches and skinny; maybe wiry would be a better description considering he hoisted my pudgy little body up off the floor in one fluid movement. Working at the gas station since he was a boy made him stronger than he looked.

When I braved the upright world, the room started spinning.

"Miss Nan, you going to hurl?" Jimmy asked.

"Not sure."

Vomiting curly fries with jalapeno flavored sea salt on his shoes, not appealing.

Claire told Laura to bring me a sandwich and a trashcan.

"Let me guess," Claire said in an agitated tone, "four curly fries are what you considered dinner tonight? Three shots of Crown on an empty stomach! You know better than that. You scared the hell out of all of us."

The "all of us" Claire spoke for included her, Jimmy, Laura, a couple playing pool, and Mutt. Mutt was a Labrador/Chow mix and a good guard dog in his heyday. Recently he seemed more interested in napping by the fake fireplace, licking up food bits dropped on the floor, and playing with my cats when they came for a visit. I apologized to everyone. Mutt came over to sniff me and looked under the table for the cats.

"Sorry, Mutt. I didn't bring your kitties tonight."

Talking didn't come easy to me after an episode. I noticed someone unplugged the music. An eerie quiet filled the room.

Claire requested, "Laura, honey, bring over one of Nan's migraine pills I keep in the back of the cash register drawer."

Turning back to me she continued her scolding. "JD is running late. He'll be in the kitchen burning fries soon enough, but you need to get something in your stomach."

"How did you know I had a headache?" I asked.

"Something about you taking an unscheduled nap on the bar-room floor might have given me a clue," she smirked.

"You look spooked, Nan," Laura said.

She handed me a half a pimento cheese sandwich, so the Midrin wouldn't hit the empty pit called my stomach. I didn't know Claire kept meds on reserve for me. Probably Harvey's idea. Any other night, I might have gotten angry about the protection detail. Tonight my gratitude outweighed my mad.

"What happened?" Jimmy asked.

My eyes wandered to the unread deck of cards. "Bête Noire," I said. "It means the 'black beast' in French."

Before they could ask me what I meant, I stuffed another bite of the cheese sandwich in my mouth and chewed. I didn't tell them this was the third time the Lady of Nightmares had visited me. The first time was the night before my father committed suicide. The second time, she came the morning my Doc killed himself.

Perhaps a visit from the dark lady only accompanied murder or suicide. I'd had no notice from Death before my mother's departure. But then when Mama died, the world felt soft and quiet. Like many of the animals I held in my arms for their last moments at the vet clinic . . . a final breath, a sigh of relief, then peace.

And piss. In death, everything lets go.

When Mother passed away, my brother Zach and I were cuddled on her bed, holding her in our arms. Pictures of Bradley and Edward were on the rolling stainless steel table pulled up close to us. My other brothers tried to get home in time. Mama drifted away as we whispered, "I love you" into her ears. She died two months after we found what was once Doc in what was once our bedroom. Fifty shades of red, not grey. I still had a pot of daffodils from Doc's funeral blooming on Mama's dinning room table when she died.

"Honey, you're drifting again." Claire snapped her fingers near my ear.

"Do you want me to drive you home?" Jimmy asked.

I didn't know what to say to Jimmy. If my insights were truthful, he would not be alive tomorrow. If I rode with him, would his destiny change for the better or worse? Would taking me home put him on a collision course with the Death Dragon? I didn't answer him.

"You feeling better?" Laura asked.

Death By Catgut

"Nothing that a Happy Meal and a Diet Coke couldn't fix," I answered.

"I'll go get it for you," Jimmy volunteered.

Yes, Angel Falls was big enough for a McDonald's, a Wal-Mart, and Jimmy's gas station, a few antique shops, a health food and a grocery store. Actually, Mickey D's lived inside the Wal-Mart.

"Hey, hey, this *is* a bar and grill," hollered JD from the kitchen.

I caught only part of him in my peripheral vision. He wrapped an apron around his waist. JD was Claire's current boyfriend and fry cook.

"I have plenty of food here," chided Claire. "Make sure that cheese sandwich stays down first."

A clash of thunder rattled the floorboards. The B & G's lights flickered. I did my best to suppress a shudder. The music on the jukebox hiccupped and started playing again on its own.

"Damn it." Claire pulled her iPhone from her pocket, and checked the world outside our conclave. "If anyone is leaving, now's the time to go. If not, I hope you all brought toothbrushes. There's a spring storm coming this way pushing hail in front of it."

Claire repeated the weather report for Milton and his

date, while they finished playing a game of Snooker. He paid his tab and left tugging the girl out the door. I didn't remember her name. Apparently, they came in while I explored the intricate, hidden designs on the B & G's wooden floor.

See there. It's the face of Elvis in the wood grain. Or is that an image of the Virgin Mary? It's difficult to decipher metaphysical art.

"Jimmy, is it okay with you if we finish your reading another time? Maybe we could sit and talk for a while to help clear my head? Or do you need to get home before the hail comes?"

"I'm not on the scooter tonight. I got my dad's pickup running. Nothing can hurt that old thing."

I managed a weak smile.

"I'll get some more curly fries since JD showed up." Jimmy's voice dropped into a whisper. "Claire burnt the first batch, but I didn't want to hurt her feelings."

"Next time try catsup. It hides a multitude of culinary sin," I raised my voice after him and immediately regretted the noise reverberating in my head.

I reached for the Tarot spread trying to be nonchalant about it. I wanted to see the last card. I held my breath and flipped the Ultimate Outcome over. The Falling Tower. A dragon with broken wings lay at the base. There was rarely a positive aspect to this card. Even in the upright position it meant a forced reassessment of beliefs and lifestyles. I shivered and quickly shuffled all the cards back into the deck before anyone could notice.

The night felt long and slow. Jimmy and I talked off and on, but mostly sat in the quiet contentment of each other's company. His stillness upset me. It was unlike him.

What could I say? What should I say? Be careful?

Claire busied herself with weekly bookkeeping. Two other customers braved the drizzle and threat of ice shards. Each ordered take-out and headed for shelter. Claire let JD and Laura go home at ten. Mutt didn't like loud weather. He hid behind the prow in the bar so Laura couldn't leash him and drag him out into the rain.

Claire told Laura, "I'll bring Mutt along later."

Laura lived in Claire's garage apartment while going to college.

"It's a bit of a drive to school," she told me once. "But hey, you can't beat free room and board."

Besides, she liked working with her aunt. They shared Mutt's care and affection. It was not unusual for Mutt to sleep at the bar, but he'd been banned from the kitchen area by a baby gate. There was a stolen steak incident for which he'd not yet been forgiven.

By midnight Claire was ready to close up. "I've wasted more money on electricity than I've made in sales tonight. What say we all call it quits?"

"Fine by me," I answered.

When Jimmy offered to drive me home again, I said, "No thanks." I told him I needed the cool, damp, night air to keep the headache at bay. I hugged him goodbye for what I thought might be the last time and held on for longer than I intended.

"Be careful of the rain naiads," I said, "They're like mermaids. They enjoy capturing strong, young men to make them their love slaves."

"Love slave?" Jimmy grinned big enough to make both his dimples show.

I waved goodbye and repeated, "Be careful."

The witching hour was aptly named tonight. Wind howled around the building corners and down the side street of our little town. The thunder made me jumpy, but at least no hail materialized. The storm turned out to be more drizzle than raging torrent. Belligerent ice shards never came. Soggy by the time I got to my back door from the light sprinkle and the heavy fog, I shook splattering droplets about. My normal furry greeting party was absent.

Gloom outside and in.

Harvey had left the radio on again, and Susan Boyle's version of "Wild Horses" played softy in the background. Seeing Doc's visage tonight upset me more than I wanted to admit. I hadn't been expecting him. Not tonight and not when we met. A flash of lightening brightened the midnight sky. In the few seconds it took for the thunder to follow, my mind got "dragged away" to a time before the lies.

It's not like I'd given up on love, I just wasn't looking for romance when Doc appeared in my life. My dance card was full with taking care of Mom and my mini-menagerie, which consisted at the time of three cats, a pot-bellied pig, and the occasional rescue/foster dog. I didn't think there was any space for an amorous relationship, but fate had other plans. The good doctor stumbled into the Angel Falls Vet Clinic with a wounded stray in his arms.

When our eyes met my heart skipped a beat. "Maybe it's my murmur acting up," I thought, trying to remember to breathe.

"Can you help me?" He blinked back tears as he handed the cur mix over to me, and cracked my heart for the first time.

Naomi Patterson

A tall, mysterious stranger with dark hair and hazel eyes crying over a wounded dog, I didn't stand a chance.

"He was lying on the side of the road. I couldn't leave him there. Maybe a car hit him, I don't know. I didn't feel any broken bones. I'll pay for whatever medical services he needs."

I managed a smile while trying not to gawk at him. The man, not the dog, "We'll do a routine check and x-ray her."

"Her?"

"Yes."

"I'm a retired dentist . . . I generally dealt with the other end of things."

I actually giggled. I tried to cover it by clearing my throat and almost choked. I think I startled the poor dog.

"She's favoring her right leg. Why don't you have a seat, Doc. I'll take her to the back, and let you know what we find in a few minutes."

Through the door and out of his sight, I gulped in air. Dr. Word looked up from her paperwork.

"What have we here?"

"The most beautiful man in the world is sitting in our lobby."

"I meant the dog. In your arms."

When I didn't respond Dr. Word gently took the dog

from me and headed for an examination table.

"Nan, I swear I've never seen this before."

Shocked back to the moment, my concern rose. "The dog?"

"No, you. I believe you're smitten."

Oh, so smitten.

It took Doc nearly eight weeks to ask me out, but he came by my house every few days to check on Fleabag's progress, not ever coming in, just passing by. When he did finally call, he made clear he wasn't asking me on a date. At his age he didn't date. He was new in town, and didn't know many people, and thought I might be better company than a magazine over dinner.

"Geez, with an offer like that how can I refuse. Would that be Newsweek, GQ, Mad or Cosmo? I'm going to need to know how to dress. You're not an Animae fan are you? I don't have a leather bustier."

He stammered for a comeback, and I feared my smart-ass attitude had put him off.

He chuckled, "No leather, hey. We'll have to fix that."

Everything that came to mind as a response was so inappropriate. Images of his athletic body in a white poet's shirt and tight fitting black leather pants raced through my mind. I bit my tongue and waited for him to speak, again.

"I want to thank you for taking such good care of Fleabag and for finding her a, what is it you call it, a Forever Home. I don't have room in my condo for pet. Anyway, I'd like to take you out to dinner."

"Sure. I love free food."

I was temporarily a blond at that juncture in my life, and Claire came over to help me touch up my roots and get ready for my "not date." The most important night of my life, and we turned my hair a slight shade of purple.

"We put too much dauber to damp down the red, I think. The good news is you're not pink."

"Not pink? Claire, I have purple hair. I have purple hair!"

She dug through my bathroom drawers and the medicine cabinet for a solution. "Why don't you witch it away? You're good with potions."

"Obviously not. I'm good with herbs. There's a difference. Basil and lavender won't fix this. I'm already lavender!"

"It's not the most unusual color you've had. I remember one year when you belonged to the color-of-the-month club. That was interesting."

I gave her the stare, but my lower lip began to quiver.

"Hey, hey, don't you dare cry. It took us forty-five minutes to do your make-up. It's the age of big hair. Give me that can of hair spray."

We manage to fluff and tease most of the lilac shade into hiding.

"Maybe the restaurant will be dark," I hoped.

"Honey, that little black dress is low-cut enough, and your ta-tas are big enough, that I'd be surprised if his gaze made it up that high."

"If I get through this night, I'm going to dye."

"What?"

"I'm going back to my natural color."

Claire snicker. "Do you even remember what that is?"

I punched her in the arm. When I came into the living room Mama smiled for the first time in a week.

"You look beautiful, my darling baby girl. But you're showing a lot of who-ha."

I looked down at my crotch.

"Higher," Claire instructed.

I tugged at my top. Claire herded Mom and her walker into the kitchen to fix her a cup of tea, throwing me finger kisses over her shoulder. Mom stopped and put our pot-bellied pig in her walker basket.

"Henrietta needs a snack too. Besides we don't want Nan's 'gentleman caller' to see a pig first thing." Mom continued to mumble all the way down the hall. "It's been a long time since Nannie's had a date. I don't understand why. She's a pretty girl, when she wants to be. Does her hair look purple to you? Maybe it's just my eyesight."

Five minutes later I opened the door to my fantasy man. He didn't move for a long moment. He just stared at me. I thought about slamming the door, and putting a paper bag over my head, then I heard him.

"Lucky me."

I asked him years later when our "not date" turned into a lifetime for him? He told me, "The moment you opened the door."

I think we ate Italian that night. I only remembered him, his eyes, his smile, his hands holding my face when he kissed me goodnight. I wrapped my leg around his calf, and felt a shiver of pleasure ripple through his body. From then on we were never apart for more than three days. We were impossibly suited for one another physically, emotionally, even spiritually. In our twelve and a half years together we only had three arguments. I couldn't tell you what they were about, silly, stupid stuff that didn't go to bed with us. He was my renaissance man: warrior spirit in a healer body, retired, gym training, knife making, piano playing, prankster who enjoyed hiding a fart machine under my table at Thanksgiving. The first time he played "Für Elise," for me, I wept. Middle-aged when we met each other, we joked about having made most of our mistakes on other people. I called him my "Shining Knight in Tarnished Armor."

"Does that make you my 'Damsel in Distress'?" he asked.

Should I have known my answer would become, "yes?" Would I have changed anything if I did?

Those once playful images and our tainted titles survived long after him. He was my heart's haven, but I was his . . . what? In our time of joy, he called me his "Sweetness."

I am different, now. I am bittersweet.

I walked into the Hilltop kitchen, from the mud-room, intent on brewing myself a cup of tea. The veil felt thin tonight, and I kept toeing the boundaries between light and dark memories. The rain fell steady but not producing the promised storm. I traced a raindrop down the pane and remembered the most romantic day of my life.

A spring rain like this one started early. I loved to walk

in the rain, Doc not so much. He enjoyed my antics and watched me dance in the drizzle on many occasions from the dry security of his front porch. For whatever reason he decided to joined me.

We wandered hand-in-hand down by the old lumberyard. In the back a shallow stream forked to create a small island in the woods that remained. We climbed down an embankment and crossed to the isle in ankle high water. We laughed. We always laughed when we were together. This little acre had been left to grow wild. It smelled and felt like stepping into a Garden of Eden. Lush, rich, green. Despite the fact that the wind chill continued to drop as the storm grew, we immediately threw off our clothes and played Adam and Eve.

The smell of the earth mulch beneath me blended with Doc's musky scent and created a heady aroma that overwhelmed me. Steam rose from his bare skin and dissipated into the grey sky. Our body heat kept me cocooned in warmth as his arms kept me protected. The birds quieted. I heard individual raindrops hitting leaves, the soothing sounds of his breath increasing, and my own heart pounding. I lost myself to our loving in this primeval forest. When I came back to myself I recognized concern on Doc's face.

"What?"

"Sweetness, I think we best be on our way home. It's

been raining hard." He gave me a wicked grin, "And we've been here a long time."

I pulled him back down. "Not long enough."

He kissed me deeply, forced himself away, and tossed clothes at me. "I'm serious. We're on an island; such as it is, surrounded by water. Old creek beds like the little one around us can rise with surprising speed."

I didn't argue. I shook leaves out of my shirt and dressed. Besides I was hungry. We had been here a goodly amount of time. He cleared branches for me to pass. I grabbed at his butt. He looked fine in tight fitting, soggy jeans. When we got back to where we had crossed, what was initially ankle-high had swollen to waist-high on me.

Doc took me by the shoulders. "We don't know how strong the current is. There could be an undertow. If I lose my footing, do not try to rescue me. You get to the other side and wait for me. I'll find my own way. Or, if not, go get your cousin to rescue … retrieve my body down stream."

What could I say, "Okay?"

I had no idea what could, and did happen next. Three steps in I got swept away. Doc lunged for me and kept me from playing "dunk the witch." I clung to him like a rhesus monkey. My added weight allowed him to wade us both across, not without considerable effort. We crawled up the hill grabbing roots, stems, rocks, anything that would hold. The easy sloop we'd sauntered down hours ago washed away in a rush of water.

Safe on higher ground, I kissed his hand. "You saved my life."

I didn't understand his wistful expression until the next day when two-dozen, bright yellow daffodils were delivered, along with a note that read, "Sweetness. It is you who has saved my life. You are my Forever Home. I love you."

That was when he cracked my heart the second time. Seven years together, at that moment, and the feelings kept growing deeper, richer, more fulfilling. He wasn't perfect, just perfect for me. I scratched a patch on my arm. A postscript attached on the back of the card read: "Enclosed is a bottle of calamine. We're going to need it."

And we did need the lotion and steroids. As a corollary to our romantic interlude, dramatic rescue, and declaration of love eternal, we discovered we were covered, totally covered, in poison ivy. For the next two weeks we air kissed because every time we touched one another, we created another rash spot. We never explained how we got "exposed" to so much of that nasty weed. We only giggled and blushed, and mumbled something about "The Curse" of Eden.

Death By Catgut

I love the man, still and again.

We managed around Mama's diminishing capacities, my work, and Doc's hobbies to create a happy life together. Doc asked me to marry him three months into our relationship, and I said "yes." He felt he had shown remarkable restrain by not asking me to be his wife on our first night together. We both knew with my mother's health issues an actual marriage was not possible unless I institutionalized her. Not an option for me. We settled into our "not marriage" with comfort and contentment. I looked forward to growing old with him by my side. Over the course of years we chose the term "life partner" to describe who we were to others. It felt right. It was right, until he broke our lives and cracked my heart for the final time.

Where did I leave the Jack Daniels?

Naomi Patterson

Dead Kings Walking

In the east hallway on the second floor at Seven Hilltop Street, I hung pictures: big, small, framed, or thumbtacked in place. They were my time capsule, my family altar, my sanctuary, my asylum. One of my favorite photos was of me dressed as the blue-winged tooth faerie. Taken at a Halloween gala at Claire's Bar and Grill, too many years ago to admit, we all looked so young. Doc came to the party as a vampire, complete with custom-made fangs. Claire wore a cave-woman outfit and wielded a wooden club. Harvey had on big pink bunny ears. Harvey told everyone he appeared as himself. He even managed a Jimmy Stewart impersonation.

My brothers' picture area needed updating. Brad had been married, divorced, and married again. Edward was expecting his first grandchild. None of those changes were apparent on my wall. I didn't have any recent pictures of Zach either, but I taped up some of the postcards he sent me from his adventures in London, Monte Carlo, Kuala Lumpur, "De Nile," and more recently California. I'd hung up a pretty picture of Mama, taken on her eighty-eighth birthday and even a small one of my whole family before Daddy died. My lover's memorial photo stood center stage, all thirteen by nineteen inches of him. I'd stroked Doc's face so many times it amazed me that the glass hadn't worn thin.

Sometimes I tell him I miss him, other times I hiss at him. It's not how he left, but what he left behind that hurt. Lies change everything.

A little past three in the morning Harvey found me sitting on the floor in our hall of memories. "What ya doing?" he asked, as if he didn't know.

"Looking at my life," I sighed.

"That's a good idea. Let me see, it usually goes something like: review-remember-regret-regurgitate. Right?"

"Something like that," I admitted. "Nice alliteration. You got into a rhythm." I wouldn't hide things from Harvey. Probably couldn't if I tried. He'd held my hair back while I vomited up my sorrows more times than any girlfriend had.

"You're not sleeping much." He stated the obvious.

"Tis the season." I poured a jigger of Jack in my coffee

cup and offered Harv the half-empty bottle. We toasted each other, and then we toasted the faces on the wall. He had pictures up there too.

"Ah, spring. It's an ironic time of year, isn't it?" He made it a rhetorical question. "Everything around us bursting back into life, while you and I 'ring out our dead.' You, a dead almost-husband. Me, my wasted youth."

"Oh, poor you," I said. "Be kind, I had a rough night."

"Dancing naked on tabletops, again?"

"Not so much. I put Crown on an empty stomach."

Harvey glared at my mug of liquor.

"I've eaten since then."

"It is the middle of the night," he said.

"Really? And here I thought we needed a new light bulb."

He slapped me on the back of my head. "It's coming up on his death anniversary, and you are preparing the annual self-sacrifice to the altar of The Great Doctor. Can I say crumpled on the floor of a bar is not a good look for you?"

Obviously, Claire called Harvey. I ignored him to stare at my homage-montage wall.

"Doc's dead," Harvey continued. "A real fantasy, now. He's the ultimate man in unavailability."

Death By Catgut

I swirled the whisky in my cup, and chugged the remainder. "I'm not afraid of ghosts. Dead kings walking about the castle are common in my family."

"You know, when he died is when you started drinking in the twilight zones," Harvey reproached.

"No," I disagreed. "After his suicide I stopped caring how much I drank, not where I drank." I gave him my best semi-loaded, sarcastic smirk.

"Why?" He'd heard the answer before, but asked anyway. "Why do you do this?"

"Abandonment, death, betrayal." I stated with the hollowness of long suffering. "Pretty much in the order I discovered them."

"His duplicity. Not yours."

Harvey was my life-long friend, champion. He'd have followed Doc to the ever after and kicked his butt if he thought it would lift my sorrow; but Harv's tolerance for fools was low.

"Doc's death didn't hurt me so much as his post-mortem confession. He screwed around on me with an old college girlfriend." I spread my arms like I was reading a marque: "Mrs. Melody Burrow, Barlow, Bungalow. She was one of those 'b' words."

"I know. Look on the bright side. You didn't get dumped

for a trophy wife."

"Not funny." I punched him hard on his thigh.

"He spent a couple of weekends with a worn-out fantasy, enjoying her family money."

"Don't patronize me," I told him. "Note to the world: If you're going to kill yourself, toss your computer in the river first."

"You could have hit the delete button."

"No, I couldn't have. I really couldn't."

"You gloss over the fact that Doc became deeply depressed the last year of his life. He was not the same man you fell in love with. You were a faithful, loving companion to the *bitter* end. Note my emphasis on bitter. Trying to kill yourself annually by accidental alcohol poisoning is not going to change anything, and it's not healthy."

I sniggered, "No shit."

"Nan, damn it. Time to move on. You've taken a twelve-year relationship and turned it into a lifetime of sorrow."

"He made a year-and-a-day vow with me, on his honor."

"Sure, sure," Harvey breathed heavily. "A Celtic promise, a soul bond, an unbreakable vow."

"Doc promised he would never lie, he would never cheat, and he would never hurt me," I whined.

Death By Catgut

"News flash: Doc did lie. He did cheat. He did hurt you. But this," he pointed to our dreary surroundings. "This is on you. Doc lied to this Mel person, too. She got caught in his chaos as well."

"DO NOT DEFEND HER. Melody had a choice. I did not. She went forward into a relationship willingly, and with full knowledge of the pain it would cause her husband, her son, me, our families. And she didn't give a crap." I ground my teeth. "Her 'yes' to his 'do you want to' destroyed my future."

Harvey sighed, "You have a future, darling. Doc is the only one who gave up that option."

"Back off. I'm not in the mood." I grabbed the Jack Daniels back from Harvey and poured more in my mug. Rather than giving him the bottle this time, I set it beside me. "Wonder what her son would think of *Mommy Dearest* if he knew she was a home wrecker?"

"Wonder what you want, but her home's not wrecked. She's married to the same husband. She's living in the same million-dollar house. She's a pillar of her community and a deacon in her church, suffering no apparent consequence to her lifestyle. Her son, her husband, her family and friends are none the wiser for her sexploits."

"How do you know?"

"You're not the only one who can navigate the Internet. She's doing fine, while you sit all alone, in a dark hallway drinking whiskey out of a cracked coffee mug."

"I'm not alone. You're here." My attitude changed from sad to hurt to angry and back to sad. I quieted.

"Missing the man, or the life that can no longer be?" Harvey asked, not unkind.

"Both." I whimpered. "When Mel took a close look at Doc, she went running home, indifferent to his distress. There was not a single phone message from her on any of his house or cell phones the entire three weeks he lay rotting on our bedroom floor. No emails – nothing."

"This isn't helping you."

"Mel wasn't there for him when he needed her, and because of her, I wasn't there either. I don't know if I can ever forgive her for that. I don't know if I can forgive me. She failed him, utterly, in every way a human being can fail another, and he failed me. Who did I fail, Harvey? Who did I fail?" I sounded like a petulant child.

"Yourself," he stated with no judgment.

"It's not fair."

"It rarely is." Harvey slid down the wall and sat next to me.

Death By Catgut

Sammie, our elder black and white cat, dragged a lap quilt from the sofa over for me. Coated in dust bunnies by the time she got it all the way down the hall, I thanked her nonetheless. Harvey pulled the comforter tight around me.

Got to love cat gifts: blankets and bird feet.

"It's you that goes to bed with a box of ashes and too many cats to count, not her. No doubt Melody has her own regrets," he suggested.

"I can only hope."

Harvey tweaked my nose. He kissed his fingers and stretched his long arm across the hallway to affectionately touch the picture of his youngest sister. She died around the same time as Doc and Mama. Colon cancer. I had been too caught up in my own sorrow to share much of his loss. I went to her funeral, I think. Seemed like I had a front row ticket at the funeral home that year. I remembered pinning a white rose on Harvey suit lapel, but that could have been for any of the services. He was an honorary pallbearer for all three.

"Death always comes in threes," I muttered.

"Superstitious nonsense," exclaimed Harv. "You either have to wait for the third event or disregard the fourth."

I ignored his pronouncement. I didn't have a lot of memories from that period in my life. A small mercy, that. Only vague images of wearing black, and kicking Kleenex boxes out of the way remained. Harvey and I packed up too many households that year. I did remember finding a tiny, sleeping orange kitten in a basket on my bed the day after we moved into Hilltop. Punkin was barely five or six weeks old, and not fully weaned. I bottle-fed her, clung to her. I'm not sure her tiny paws touched the floor for the next month.

"They all leave, eventually." My housemate stared at pictures on our hall wall, lost in memories of his own.

"Who?" I asked.

"Everything, everyone we love . . . people, pets, plants. They all die. Nothing lasts forever, Nan."

Considering how much Jack I'd had and my puncheon for sarcasm, it amazed me that I skipped right over the loving a plant part. "Wow. That's cynical for you."

"I have my moments," he admitted, like a confession rather than a joke.

"All these years after, and I still feel stupid," I said. "I had no idea what was going on. I thought he was dealing with normal mid-life issues, and would be home by the Fourth of July. Stupid, stupid, stupid."

I hit myself in the head with the coffee mug to emphasize my point. Harvey stopped me with a gentle hand.

"This other woman lived five states away. It's not like Doc popped out at lunch to get some. Look, the guy was a genius, a high functioning sociopath, clinically depressed, and very good at hiding his bad behavior." Harv tried to comfort me in his odd way.

"You don't understand betrayal. I suppose I should be grateful that you don't." I reached for the shredded tissue tucked in my sleeve. "Sometimes when I think about him, I can't breathe."

"Stop thinking about him," Harvey instructed. "Stop. Thinking. About. Him. And Her. Doc is dead, and Mel of no consequence. She is a woman with few morals and no ethics."

I sniffed, "There's a difference?"

"Yes. Her morals told her what she and Doc were doing was hurtful and wrong, but her ethics, or rather lack thereof, allowed her not to care about the consequences for her family or you."

I leaned my head on Harv's shoulder.

He continued, "There are several people, not to mention a few beasties, that need you."

"The big 'why' will never get answered. I accept that, most days, but I wish, just once, Melody had said she was sorry. A simple little, 'I'm sorry I hurt you.' Instead I got lies, lies, and more lies. She told me they were 'only old friends'."

"Did you ever allow for that as a possibility?"

I cocked my head in Harv's direction, and looked at him as if he were an alien. "Emails swearing their undying love to one another and a naked photo montage of her in Doc's computer took that illusion from me. She blamed everything on him."

"It takes two people," said Harvey.

I interrupted him. "I get that. That very information is what keeps me up at night, drinking in my hallway, staring at pictures of a dead man."

"I'm sorry they both hurt you."

"Thanks, but it's not the same. I wish I hadn't found out about the affair. It sounds ugly, but I wish Doc had killed himself before he was unfaithful to me."

"I wish I may, I wish I might, have the wish I wish tonight."

I kissed his hand. We sat for a long moment in silence.

"Maybe Doc did what he could in his madness to protect you," Harvey suggested.

"What are you talking about?" I asked incredulously.

"Maybe he hid the worst of himself from you. He never acknowledged this Mel person to anyone – not a single friend or family member knew about the affair."

"She was married, Harvey. It was a secret."

"When a man is in love with a woman, he doesn't hide it. He tells the world."

"You quoting song lyrics to me now?"

"Your widow's endowment from Doc paid off this house. We found your pictures on his walls when we cleaned out his condo, your pictures in his wallet, by his bed, on his refrigerator for Christ's sake. No one came and went in his home. He was a hermit. He could have plastered his walls with pictures of Mel. And yet there wasn't a single photo of her, anywhere, except a booty-call montage on his computer. Geez Nan, he died wearing your promise ring. Isn't that enough?"

I worried that same ring into a raw circle on my finger, held in place by my smaller matching band. "I don't think so," I finally answered him.

"The king is dead. Long live the Queen."

"Don't make me snort my booze." I could finally feel Jack in my system. I'd had enough.

"How long will you mourn him?"

I heard the agitation and disappointment in his voice. He was tired of Nan duty. I couldn't blame him; I was tired of me too.

"For the rest of my life," I whimpered into his shoulder. "We were handfasted. I made that vow too . . . on my life, not his."

Then the real tears came, and Harvey held me. I cried for my mother, father, Doc, Jimmy, for what was left of my fragmented life.

"I love . . ." I started, but couldn't finish.

"Sure, sure," he soothed, and patted my hair. "Maybe it's time for some new pictures on this hall wall?"

Three cats came to investigate my yowling, and snuggled in close to offer me warmth and comfort. Punkin wiggled onto my lap and purred. In a few moments, the penetrating heartache lightened. I felt only the everyday emptiness that all humans over the age of five understand.

"Look." Harvey pointed to the window at the end of the hall where hints of baby blues and carnation pinks began to blend with canary yellows and sprays of morning orange. "We made it through another night." He whispered softly into my hair as he kissed the top of my head. "It's Saturday. Time for all us creatures of the night to get some sleep."

He shuffled me into my room, took my shoes off, and tucked five of the cats and me into bed. Punkin snuggled into my armpit and tickled me with her whiskers.

Death By Catgut

"Thank you."

"You're welcome. Sweet dreams and cat tails up your nose," Harvey said, leaving my door ajar for paw traffic.

The last sound I remembered was purring rain.

Naomi Patterson

Pussyfooting

I woke up sometime after mid-day, upside down and backwards in my bed with the sheets tangled around my legs trapping me like an unwanted lover's arms. No cat tails in my nose. My ever-loyal Punkin, managed to stay curled in my armpit while Fidget and Twilight were doing their orange and black version of a yin/yang symbol by my feet. Max and Cricket, the copycat, were on sentry duty. Cricket, a tiny black shorthair, tailgated the big Siamese everywhere he went.

I heard the "dynamic duo" brushing past my partially opened window on one of their loops around the house. They made the circuit outside, on a foot-wide ridge around the second floor. The wrought-iron filigree made the ledge look like a dollhouse version of a widow's walk. Hilltop's third level was designed as half-a-floor build-out with a rooftop balcony. The door going out of Harvey's man-cave (or should it be man-loft?)

stuck shut from old paint and wet weather. We got to the wanna-be party terrace with a ladder through a hole in the second story roof.

Roof repairs are on the list to fix, after two new water heaters but before painting. The big blue tarp over the hole makes the third floor look like it's hiding a dead giant's body.

We had no overnight guests at the vet clinic, so I did not have to go in and feed anyone. My Saturday would be my own unless an emergency case phoned in. The single appointment we had on the books at work was midwifing the birth of a foal. The mare wasn't due until midweek.

"Come on. The day's half wasted," I announced to my bedmates.

Since none of my bed partners seemed overly concerned or excited about moving. I crawled around the edge of the queen-sized bed trying not to disturb the three catnappers. I indulged in a long semi-hot shower. Phizner and Ashley, our greys, were water babies. They joined me splashing at the bubbles from my shampoo. I tore myself from the soothing warmth of the rain forest showerhead Harvey installed, at my request, when my stomach growled for breakfast. After dressing in my yardwork capris and grabbing my hat, I headed downstairs.

Harvey would already be off to the H.E.B. by this time of day, and as usual he left a cold pot of coffee waiting for me to nuke when I wandered into the kitchen. He neatly folded the *Angel Falls Chronicle* by my place at the table with an empty cup and a day old cinnamon bun wrapped in aluminum foil. Sammie would chew through plastic wrap to get to sweet rolls, so we had to take extra precautions.

The *Chronicle* came out twice a week, Saturdays for coupons, and Wednesdays for the rest of the town announcements. If no real news presented, sometimes the *Chronicle* skipped a mid-week print. "If it bleeds, it leads*"* even in a small town. After what I'd seen in Jimmy's card reading last night, I feared what the headlines might be. I did not want to find a story about Jimmy's death covering the front page, so I left the paper untouched. The phone rang.

"Hello, Pussyfoot Bed and Breakfast," I answered, recognizing Claire's cell number on caller ID.

"That's not a bad idea. You and Harvey have the space. Harvey's a good cook, but you'd have to change it to Dinner and a Pillow with your schedule. You are not a natural-born early riser," Claire said.

"As a general rule, cats sleep late. Hey, we offer a cocktail hour as a concierge service. You'll have to ignore cat hair, in, on, or around you. If catnip and cream is not to your liking, I make a mean Pussy Willow."

"I'm a bartender, but I've never heard of that," Claire admitted.

"Harv made it up. It's like a Grasshopper, but not green. He uses clear Crème de Menthe, White Crème de Cacao, Vodka, a splash of green Tabasco and sparkling water, and then stirs it with a branch from a Pussy Willow. When my roomie is being really creative, he makes willow branches out of marzipan and white chocolate."

"I'm a Crown woman through and through, but that actually sounds good, especially the chocolate part." Claire changed the subject to a more serious tone. "How are you? I don't mean your head, I mean your heart?"

The empty airspace started to suffocate me.

"You want the politically correct version or the truth?" I bent to pick up scattered pieces of kitty kibbles knocked out of the bowls, sat down on the floor, and leaned against the kitchen cabinet for support.

"Both, if they're different," Claire said.

I banged the back of my head against the wood door.

"What the hell is that noise?" she asked.

I lied. "The cats."

"And?" she prompted.

"And, I'd rather not be here, Claire." I answered truthfully.

"Move," she suggested without sarcasm.

I had to be careful what words I used. Claire sat suicide watch for me during and after my year of all things dying. "I rather not be anywhere on this particular planet. I'm feeling like it's time to be elsewhere."

"Let's see: you're not eating, you're not sleeping, you're drinking a lot, even by my standards, and the only goals you have left in life are picking asparagus out of the garden and reading the *Twilight* saga. Skip reading book number two in the mood you're in."

What is it with middle-age women and vampires?

"There's some early basil and lavender to harvest," I laughed to lighten the mood, but my voice came out like a cackle.

"Can't we do some sort of goodbye -- good riddance ritual?" she asked, sincerely. "You know, get you past all these maudlin anniversary issues? You like rituals. We'll start with some red wine. You can call it dragon's blood."

"Dragon's blood?"

"Yeah. We'll pull out a picture of your mom, and you

can tell her you love her," Claire continued. "We'll toast her with some dragon's blood Zinfandel. Then we'll walk out back to the pet cemetery, and you can place some basil and lavender on the graves."

"So, you are listening when I babble herb lore." I tried to stop her litany but failed.

"Once we're done with the small ghosts, we'll open a bottle of dragon's blood Sauvignon. We'll take Doc down from the bookshelf, or out from under your bed, wherever you're keeping the SOB these days. We'll put a handful of him in the litter boxes, to make a point, and dump the rest of his crazy ash in the woods behind the house. It'll help, I promise. And we'll finish by drinking, wait for it . . . some dragon's blood Pinot Noir. Girlfriend, I'll introduce you to a 'Day of the Dead' celebration like you've never experienced. We'll make it one big 'Fare Thee Well' to all."

"Thank you for your sentiment."

I felt worse for my predawn encounter with Jack and didn't want to argue with her. Between my family, my housemate's hobby, and the vet clinic, I was on a first-name basis with the Grim Reaper. I called him Grimmy when it's only the two of us. I didn't need an introduction and I didn't want a party.

"It's not a box of ashes that hurts me. Doc's betrayal left ugly scars in my mind and on my heart. I'm not sure I'll ever heal."

"Bullshit! Get over it, Nan. People live with broken hearts all the time. You are not the only walking wounded in the world."

Excuse me, I'm getting attitude from everyone.

I heard her light up and puff on her Virginia Slim. I didn't have to be a psychic to realize something was wrong.

"Walk your self-pitying ass over here. I need help. And bring those two orange monster-sized cats of yours. Mutt is driving me crazy. He needs someone to play with or chew on."

She hung up before I could ask more. I'd been summoned in a most unusual way. I changed my garden clogs for sneakers and put Mittens and Marmalade in their halters and leashes. Many of our kitties walked on leashes. Not Twilight. She did an alligator death-roll when we tried to put even a collar on her. M & M, however, knew the drill. When I rattled their harnesses and shouted "Bar and Grill," they came running like Punkin did when I yelled "Garden."

We marched toward Claire's. The three of us didn't get stares from the locals anymore. Tourist season was different. Vacationers often snapped photos of the crazy lady and her ambassador cats, especially when I wore my pointed hat.

No traditional greeting met me when we entered Claire's fine establishment. I unhooked the cats without speaking. They both jumped Mutt who, obligingly, rolled on his back to wrestle.

After taking a seat, I broke the silence, "What's up?"

"Jimmy's missing."

Lost and Found

"Missing?" I couldn't look Claire in the eyes. *Maybe if I'd told him what I saw in his cards, maybe if I'd let him give me a ride home, maybe he wouldn't be missing?* I felt like I was going to throw up.

"It doesn't look like Jimmy made it home last night." Claire poured me a shot of Crown. "You eat today?"

I nodded, and she made it a double, but she poured me a glass of Diet Coke as well.

"After last night's episode, you better mix the hard stuff. These are on the house," she said.

Everything I ate or drank was "on the house." I wondered sometimes how Claire stayed in business. I nodded my thanks and poured the Crown into the soda.

"What makes you think Jimmy never made it home?"

"Because the gas station is not open today. Laura

stopped by this morning to fill up her Vespa. It's after noon by most people's watches. No Jimmy." Claire pursed her lips to say more, but stopped.

Jimmy's family built the small station. It had been passed down through the generations. The TV filing station in old reruns of Andy Griffin's *Mayberry* looked like a modern marvel compared to Jackson's Gas-N-Go and Souvenir Shop. If you needed diesel you had to keep driving to the next larger town.

"When Laura got to the station she beeped . . . no Jimmy. So, she went to the back to see if he'd overslept. She said his little efficiency looked like it had been hit by a tornado. Laura couldn't tell if the bed had been slept in, but there was no coffee brewing out front," Claire added.

"His apartment had been ransacked?" I asked.

Not everyone locks their doors around here, but maybe it's time to start.

"Difficult to tell. He's a boy, living on his own. Might be everything has a place and that place is on the floor. But no coffee out front means Jimmy wasn't there in the morning. That worries me."

"Maybe he drove into the city to pick up supplies? There might have been a run on pecan logs and moon pies or those angel-wing keychain things he sells." I didn't believe me. I didn't think she would either.

"He wouldn't, not without getting his cousin to sub for him, or putting a 'Be Back in Ten" sort of note on the window. That station is Jimmy's life. Before you ask, I already called his cousin. Joe is down in Bayville doing day labor. I talked to Jerri Ann, the cousin's live-in. She didn't have much to say beyond 'nope' and 'yup.' I swear if that girl and Joe have children we will dumb-down and over-populate the earth in one birth."

"Be nice," I admonished.

"No reason to be," Claire quipped. "I don't know those two except to say that first impressions don't do them any kindness. Pumping gas and counting change seems to tax Joe's intellectual abilities. Brute force is his strong point."

"Not a lot of calls for gladiators these days."

"More's the pity for those of us who have to deal with his kind outside of an arena."

"You have an unpleasant encounter with Joe?"

Claire raised her hands over her head. "I'm just saying . . ."

I'd met Joe over the last couple of years when Jimmy took a sick day. Joe was older than Jimmy, by about five years and bigger. He hadn't made any impression on me. Jerri Ann was a new addition. I'd done a reading or two for her, but nothing stuck out as memorable. My breakfast sticky bun did flip-flops in my stomach. The liquor wasn't helping, but I raised my glass for another. Mutt let out a yip. The orange tag-team was winning round one. I didn't worry; if Mittens and Marmalade got too rough, Mutt would sit on them until they settled down.

"Did you call Ross?" I asked. My cousin wore the badge here-abouts.

"Didn't have to; Laura went straight over to his headquarters. Sheriff will be here in a few minutes. You and me were the last people to see and talk with Jimmy last night." She lit another cigarette. "I do believe we are suspects in his disappearance."

"That's being a bit heavy-handed. Don't you think?"

Claire pointed her cigarette hand at me and repeated, "Suspects."

"I've never been a suspect before," I sighed.

She raised her eyebrow in mock surprise.

"Not for a disappearance," I clarified.

"I'm guessing your little fainting drama last night had something to do with what you saw around the boy in those cards of yours. You getting any more of those funny feelings?"

Sadly, I said, "No." None of this felt real to me.

"What did you see?" she asked.

Before I could answer her, Ross's Jeep pulled up outside. As he walked through the door, cool, spring air rushed in with him replacing the smoke and sour beer odor. The rain last night had cleared out any leftover feeling of winter. I normally didn't notice the stale bar smell. This morning my senses were on high alert. Hangovers did that to me. Claire drew up a draft of Budweiser for the sheriff.

"Ross," she acknowledged and slid the pilsner glass in his direction.

"I'm on duty, Miss Claire."

"I know, and I'm not open for another three hours, so I'm not serving beer."

Ross took his hat off, raised his glass in thanks, and ambled toward where I hunched over my empty glass. Ross wasn't a tall man. He wasn't a short man. He was what we called "solid" in my family: five-foot eleven inches, a hundred and eighty-five pounds of muscle. A first cousin on my father's side, he had that same blend of Comanche/Irish as me with the chestnut-colored hair and beguiling blue-green eyes. Sometimes in the right light our eye color turned turquoise.

"Ladies, I suppose you know I'm here about Jimmy?"

Death By Catgut

Ross said as he sipped his beer.

"I had a slow night, Sheriff. The weather turned bad. Not much happened," Claire said. "Jimmy had a healthy appetite . . . ate two, no three servings of fries."

Ross held the chilled pilsner glass against his forehead. I wondered if he had a headache today. They ran in our family. He had an irritating way of waiting out the silence.

"I shared some curly fries with Jimmy. We started his card reading," I added.

I squirmed on my seat. I didn't want to tell my cousin about my dizzy spell. He worried about me. I opened my mouth to make up a funny story, but stopped. I could tell by the set of his brow Ross was not in the mood for any she-Nan-igans, as he called my misadventures. He caught me in mid-mischief all the time, and made me feel like confessing whether I'd done anything wrong or not. If he hadn't gone into the justice system, he'd have made a good principal or priest.

"Oh?" He pulled out his pad and pencil.

"Ross, get that look off your face," scolded Claire. "I only had five customers. That doesn't include Nan, Laura, JD or Mutt. Not sure why I opened at all. Jimmy came in early like he always does. He walked the floor while he ate fries and waited for Nan to show up. Milton and some girl stopped in to play pool, but they left before the storm. Nan had one of her headaches, then I sent Laura and JD home around ten."

"The other patrons?" he asked.

"Early tourists. Not locals. They ordered take-out hamburgers. Nothing special or weird."

Ross glanced back at me.

"Contrary to popular belief, weird is not my middle name," I declared.

Claire snorted, and I caught the flicker of a grin creeping onto Ross's face.

"A short break opened in the rain. Jimmy, Claire and I left at midnight," I offered.

"Jimmy left on his scooter, I drove my pickup, and Nan hoofed it to Hilltop," said Claire.

"No. Jimmy told me he got his dad's old pickup running." I added, "He offered to drive me home, but I needed to clear my head. I walked home."

"You walked home, in the rain?" Ross asked.

"In the drizzle," Claire corrected him. "The promised storm never materialized."

"No, the real storm is still to come," I thought to myself. I dropped my voice into a contralto stage whisper for dramatic effect. "I floated home on the breath of angels. I am a witch, remember?"

"Um-hum," Ross swallowed the last of his brew. "You're a vet assistant, Nan."

Claire laughed and pointed out to me, "You're mixing your mystical and mundane metaphors."

I swirled the ice in my glass of Crown and Diet Coke. "That too."

"You *feeling* anything I should know about?" Ross asked. "You said you had a spell last night."

I heard no condescension in his tone. Both Claire and I understood his meaning of "feeling." I started chewing on the skin around my thumbnail.

"More like a spill than spell. I went down and out. Not pretty."

"Not pretty at all," Claire corroborated.

I rolled my eyes at her, then turned to my cousin. It's all shadows."

He got up and hugged me. "Yeah, for me too, Cuz."

Ross knew about my visions. He never confessed to having anything more than "unsubstantiated clues" in his mind. Admitting to hearing voices or seeing things others couldn't never boded well at re-election time. Those of us in his close circle of family and friends said he was a detective of merit with astounding insight into the criminal element.

"What do we do?" I asked.

"Go door to door," Claire suggested.

Ross put his hat back on. "Officially, no one has reported Jimmy missing. He's a grown man and doesn't have to answer to anyone. We're pushing the missing persons issue. He could show up on his own, but we all know Jimmy."

"I'll hang the 'Gone Fishing' sign on the B & G door," Claire offered. "That way no one will expect us to be open. You can gather the search party here, Sheriff."

"Right now, it's not a search and rescue operation. It's going to be friends out hiking in a straight line," he glanced at me to see if I would change his intent from search and rescue to search and recovery.

I couldn't verify or validate anything. I tried not to let him see me shiver.

"Letting us gather here to get started is much appreciated, Claire. We'll begin in one hour. Nan, please give Harvey a call. Find out if he can get away from the grocery store. I'm going to holler at David. We can use both of their tracking skills. Mutt, if you leave those two cats behind, you can come too."

Mutt thumped his tail like he understood, but nosed his

buddies affectionately as Mittens crawled over his back to attack his wagging tail, and Marmalade batted at his right ear.

"Let me call JD," said Claire. "We'll have food waiting off the tailgate of my truck and I've got plenty of water bottles. We'll travel where you do and be your base."

Ross looked me straight in the eyes. "You see anything, you let me know."

I forced a smile onto my lips, and my cousin left to rally the troops. Claire offered me another shot. This time, I declined. I needed a clear head if I was actually going hunting for the dead.

Mouse Meat Pies

"We're going to need pictures of Jimmy," declared Claire. "You start a list of everything else we'll need."

While I searched for a pen or pencil, I asked, "I don't have a picture of Jimmy. Do you?"

"Here on the cork board by the clean coffee cups. Laura took it last month." She handed me the picture and a pad of paper. "One, JD needs to bring the portable generator from home. We may need light later, if we stay out past dark. Two, he needs to bring his little black bag."

"His what?" I asked.

"That cook of mine was a medic in another life, three tours in the Iraqi sandbox. If Jimmy is hurt, JD can help stabilize him until paramedics arrive. If he's not stable . . ." She changed gears.

"I didn't realize JD served," I mumbled more to myself than her.

Death By Catgut

"You're a military brat. Did you not notice the jarhead hair cut?" Claire asked.

"I thought it was hot in your kitchen," I excused my ignorance.

"Some psychic you are. Here, drink a damn shot. You've got that dead stare in your eyes."

"The whim-whams," I corrected her. "Harvey and I call it the whim-whams." I changed my mind and drank the shot. My hands were trembling.

"You have a Bug-Out-Bag packed, dear?" asked Claire.

"Yeah, but I call it my hiking backpack. Are we planning on finding Jimmy or running away?" I tried to tease, but it fell flat.

Claire grabbed the medical supplies she kept near the stove, and shoved them into a beige leather duffel bag with neon yellow straps. An expensive bag when new, it was missing a brass foot, and had been patched in two spots with "designer" duct tape. The bag was well traveled, as was its owner. Claire phoned me from one of her vacations, via satellite, in Granada asking Harv and I to run the B & G for a couple of extra evenings (before Laura was old enough to serve and run the bar). While sailing in the Caribbean, Claire had been caught in the middle of a civil war. She said she was having some "minor difficulty" getting her boat out of hostile water. My friend called herself a tropical gypsy. I think she missed the sea, but when I asked her why she came inland she laughed.

"Living on the water is highly overrated, especially in hurricane season."

There was more to the story, but I never pushed. *Some friendships are built on what you say to one another; ours grows equally out of what we don't have to.*

Claire and I were "BFFs," or "best-ies" as the kids called it, but we never talked about where she got her money. The Bar and Grill opened year round, but most of the town worked seasonal. Folks either learned to parcel out funds from the busy time to last throughout the year, or they packed up, left and returned before the tourists.

"Damn it all. We're low on bug spray," Claire exclaimed. "Even this early we'll face some creepy-crawlies out in the woods."

I didn't think she was mad at the bugs or upset at the lack of repellant. I picked up Jimmy's picture. He was smiling. Behind him, JD held a pitcher of beer over the boy's head. Laura defended him with her dishtowel. Everyone in the background laughed. I held a moment of joy in my hand. Maybe the last one Jimmy had known.

Death By Catgut

"I've got to go get my hat," I choked and stumbled toward the door. "Mittens, Marmalade, time to go home."

"Nan, stop at the CopyQuick and get fifty copies of Jimmy's picture on your way back. We'll need to pass them around. Wait. Let me write down some stats." Claire fumbled for a larger piece of paper. "James 'Jimmy' Jackson. Age: 25. Height: 5'6". Eyes: Brown. Hair: Sandy Blond. Last seen wearing a blue flannel shirt, blue denim jeans, and a Mobil Oil baseball cap."

I read her description. "How do you remember all that?" I asked. I scratched through the brown eyes and wrote in amber.

"Nannie, you see things your way, I see things mine. Don't be too long. There's a lot of work to do before we head out." She hit the numbers on her cell phone. "Where the hell is JD?"

I left her talking to herself.

"And bug spray," she hollered after me.

Harvey beat me home. Ross apparently got through to him before I did. He had his Merrell hiking boots on, and both our backpacks were ready for our journey. His Australian walking stick leaned against the dining room table. Fidget, our adolescence orange, worried the leather tassel that hung from the top of the cane.

"Your wicking tee shirt and double cotton socks are on the table. Your camper pants with the drawstrings legs are in the dryer. It's too cool for snakes, but we'll be in the brush. There'll be bugs. Your canteen has water and your flask has vodka. Try not to get them mixed up." His tone was in between an order and a request.

"Claire and JD will have water, food and field medicine," I told him.

"Don't forget your hat. I mean the purple, pointy-one. I stuck some yellow sunflowers on the brim. Jimmy is more likely to recognize you in that hat than any of us in baseball caps or cowboy hats. If he's hurt, he might make out that ratty, old thing with bright yellow flowers."

Is he referring to the hat or me when he says ratty, old thing?

Sure enough, the vase in the kitchen stood empty. In my one attempt to be a domestic goddess, I had put up flowery curtains over the sink and plopped a Mason jar stuffed with silk sunflowers on the counter. My witchy wardrobe was newly adorned with the saffron foliage. Max played with a cloth leaf Harv had dropped. The big cat watched me change my clothes. He yawned.

Middle age sucks. I can't even impress a seven-year old

cat.

By the time I finished dressing, Harvey had already walked halfway down the path toward the Bar and Grill. On the dining table an old cookbook lay open. I wondered if Harv had been in prep mode for dinner, or one of our cats had a sense of humor. The recipe showing was for Mince Meat Pies. Someone in the course of time had scratched over the title to read: Mouse Meat Pies (what you don't know won't hurt you). I slammed the book shut, and managed to startle Max and myself. I really, really, really did not want to go tromping through the woods looking for a dead body.

Dead body? No. I mean Jimmy. Happy, laughing, maybe unconscious Jimmy in the woods.

Punkin head-butted me back into the moment that mattered. We gave each other breathy kisses, and I put my hat securely on my head.

#

The usual seven volunteers from town were assembled at Claire's Bar and Grill by the time I got back with the fifty pictures of Jimmy. Sans bug spray.

Not multi-tasking today. Focus, Nannie.

There were about ten new people milling around, early tourists. Everyone wore paper namctags. Two law enforcement dogs and their handlers from the sheriff's department in the next county stood with Ross. I took solace in the fact that the two hounds were Search and Rescue, not Cadaver Dogs. The canine constables made that distinction for me on a missing child case a few summers ago, but I didn't remember their names. The gentlemen nodded cordially. I caught a smirk on the younger officer's face. It must have been the sunflower fashion statement.

When Mooch, Ross's yellow Labrador, and Mutt saw me walk in, they checked for cat companions. Finding none they went back to inspecting each other's butts and remaking their acquaintances with . . . with . . . Rocky the German Shepherd and Coco the chocolate Lab. It seemed easier for me to remember animal names than human ones. Mutt would stay behind with Claire when we began our morbid walkabout. Too old to hunt, he liked the attention of the gathering even if he didn't understand the reason.

I wish I didn't.

Sheriff Paul Ross Kelson didn't need a megaphone. His voice carried in the eerie quiet of the early afternoon. "Let me begin by saying 'thank you' for your help this afternoon. Some of you have walked a search line before, looking for a lost camper, a child or missing pet. For those newcomers who have never done an on-the-ground search and rescue, I'll go over some of the rules."

Ross tipped his cowboy hat at our old family friend and his favorite fishing buddy. "For the benefit of my friend, David Blue Sky, who's a might long in the tooth and short in the memory department, I'll keep this simple."

David spoke up in his deep baritone, "Yeah, yeah, Puppy. We'll see who gets lost in the woods."

Ross winked at David. "Hopefully, no one. We walk two arms width from each other in as straight a line as the lay of the land will allow. DO NOT STRAY. We are looking for one person today. We do not want to be looking for two. Always keep the person to your left and to your right in your sight. If the terrain becomes too rough, we will stop and reassemble. Everyone should have a walking stick, water bottle, watch, and a bandana soaked in cool water around your neck."

Ross held up his hands to forestall questions and interruptions. "The weather's chilly now, but you'll be grateful for the bandanas shortly. I recommend a flashlight, a pocketknife, and a cell phone. Please carry a picture of Jimmy with you."

Claire walked through the crowd and passed out the pictures.

"And, don't forget your hats. We walk twenty minutes and sit for five. We are pushing light this afternoon, two hours out and two back in. Claire and JD will you step forward?"

Claire took off her hat and waved it. JD tipped his ball cap as they stepped closer to the sheriff.

Ross continued, "These two folks are Control Central. You get hurt, hungry, lost, scared, or tired, send word down the line until it reaches one of the four of us officers with a walky-talky. We've got runners for emergencies." He pointed them out to the crowd. "Please, do not leave the line until the people on your left and right realize you are down. If you don't know the people walking beside you, introduce yourselves. If you quit the search to go to the bathroom, to go home, to go anywhere other than walking with us, make sure Claire and JD also know you are gone." He pulled out his cell phone and held it up. "Bring your cells if you've got 'em, but be aware that some of them don't pick up a signal in the hills. Nevertheless, here is a contact number. Please program it into your phones, in case you need it." He pointed to the number that had been written on Claire's Today's Special chalkboard. "It's the number for down at the sheriff's department. We have another volunteer, Miss Snookie Adams, manning the phones for us this afternoon."

Snookie, a retired RN, owned the health food store in

town. She was sixty-nine years old and still ran 10Ks, worked a fifty-hour week at her shop, and volunteered in her spare time.

Not sure when the woman sleeps.

"Remember to sign IN," Ross waved a yellow pad of paper in the air, "And when we get back, sign OUT. That's it. Look at your watches. Time starts now. Head toward the gas station. From there we will go up and out. Again, thanks for the help."

The macabre parade through town walked quietly. Even those who did not participate knew the purpose. Some townsfolk stood with their hands over their hearts, others turned their heads away. The town felt uneasy. The breeze stilled, and the birds went silent. Hair on the back of my arms and neck stood up.

Crap cubed.

I guessed it was a given that the crazy lady in the purple pointy hat with sunflowers sticking out everywhere was the designated body finder. At any rate, no one wanted to walk the line beside me. Harvey took my left side and Ross walked on my right. It would have been better if we had spread them into the line, but the local folks that showed up had done this before.

Nothing much happened the first hour. The rain last night had been hard enough to wash away light traces. The strangle vines hadn't taken hold, but the underbrush grew knee high in some areas. We found bobcat scat, muddy paw prints from a coyote or a wild dog, a bag of picnic trash, a pile of used condoms, and several empty wine bottles, but no Jimmy. We took more breaks because of all the newcomers.

Fine by me. I carried fifteen more pounds in my body than the last time I'd walked a line, and I felt every ounce jiggling. We had two false sightings. One turned out to be a discarded sleeping bag, and the other a pile of rubbish with a flannel shirt on top.

God bless Harv for my flask.

My housemate and Ross never looked sideways at me when I raised the silver flagon to my mouth. We continued to trample any buds of spring that poked their heads up and grew in the way of our feet. During the second hour, feet not used to walking wooded terrain began to blister. Two walking sticks snapped under the pressure. Many of the new hikers were out of water and looking like a heat stroke waiting to happen.

We sent Jason Blue Sky, David's grandson, back to base camp for more water and protein snack bars. One of the tourists apologized for dropping out and went back with him. There were about two hours of light left. Not all of that true light. This time of year we dipped into twilight around six o'clock. Those of us who knew the area could go on. David, Harvey and Ross could track all night, but there were twenty-four people to get out of the wooded area and safely back to town before dark.

At the gas station, Ross double-checked the roll call sheet. On any other day, I would have felt the need to point out my cousin's anal tendencies to him. Today, I understood it was critical to come back with as many people as we left with. Most of the search group said goodbye and went home to rub sore feet. Ross and his deputy, Ron Hastings, shook hands with each of them and thanked everyone, personally, as they left.

A smaller group of diehard community supporters would be back in the morning. I knew Ross, David, and Mooch would go back into the woods tonight. Time was not our friend. The temperature would dip to the forties with the wind-chill factor making it unkind to any unsheltered, possibly injured man or beast. Ross tipped his hat to me, and I walked over.

"How are you feeling after our walk in the woods?" My cousin asked.

"Tired."

"And?" Ross prompted.

"And tired. Jimmy could be out there, hurt, but if you're asking me if I'm *feeling*-feeling anything, the answer is no." I took my pointy hat off and wiped my brow.

Ross nodded, "Me neither. Better luck tomorrow. See you in the morning?"

"You bet. Love to hike on sunny Sunday mornings." I was being genuine though I didn't like the reason for this particular jaunt.

"Make sure Harv walks you home tonight."

I made my you-got-to-be-kidding-me face. Ross pointed two fingers at me like he directed traffic around a car wreck and gave me back his no-bullshit scowl. I scurried after my housemate.

Ross hollered at Harvey and me. "David says to bring your poncho tomorrow. Rain's coming again."

Only Ross and David can track in the rain, and maybe Jason.

I yelled over my shoulder to David, "Your shamanistic senses tingling, Chief?"

"Nope, witchy-woman. It's my weather knee." He pointed to his right leg, "Old soccer injury. It always acts up when the weather is changing."

"Should I do my anti-rain dance?" I started to jerk.

Harvey put his hands on my shoulders. "Oh no. Friends don't let friends dance, in public, when they move like you."

"It's free-form," I defended.

We all laughed. We needed to laugh. Each hour Jimmy stayed missing our chances of finding him, alive, diminished.

"You can dance in my circle any time." David grinned at me. "We'll be in rougher terrain tomorrow. No umbrellas. You may need your arms for balance."

I flashed him the two thumbs up sign.

Great. Backpacks, blisters, bugs, a leaky poncho and the promise of mud. I might need a bigger flask.

Daffy-Doodles

Dawn-thirty came early, but we didn't know how much daylight we'd have with the inclement weather looming. A smaller group than yesterday met at Claire's. JD begged off with a backache, and several of the new people didn't show up. I couldn't blame them. Tromping through the woods, in the rain, looking for a person they didn't know was not the best way to begin any spring-break activity.

Claire and I hugged. She handed me a cup of coffee. David and I hugged. He handed me an orange. Ross and I hugged. He handed me a jar of Vicks.

"Thank you?"

"Any dreams?" he asked.

I shook my head. "I was dead to the world." I winced at my choice of word. "You?"

"No." Ross wore his unemotional, professional face. He

patted my hand that held the little blue jar. "Put that in you pack."

I could name four or five uses for Vicks Vapor Rub, most of them pleasant. One, however, was to apply it to the upper lip to cover up the smell of death. Different dead things smelled different, but once the odor of human decomposition was experienced, the mind and heart never forgot it. A first responder at Doc's condo told me not to cover the odor of his death with a fragrance that I would run into anywhere in my daily routines.

"While you're cleaning out the place, don't spray your perfume in the mask or use a fabric softener sheet to breath through," he instructed. "Because if you use that same fragrance in your laundry, it will most likely cause a scent memory of this." He spread his hands to include the condo turned tomb, but he meant my sorrow as well.

Apparently, normal people didn't do well with the concept of eau d'decomp as a fashion accessory. I'm not normal, but it was kind advice. Olfactory senses connected to our primal brain. Scents triggered memories, autonomic reactions, fight or flight responses, and cognitive mechanisms designed to save our stinky, human lives. Sights might shock us, sounds could startle us, but certain smells scared the crap right out of us, sometimes literally.

Masking the odor didn't work for me. It wasn't the odor I found offensive (good thing for my taxidermist housemate); rather a taste in the back of my throat. Death left an acrid yet sweet film in my mouth, as if too much snot and Robitussin got stuck halfway down.

David had been right about the weather. We lost most of our second day of searching to rain. We didn't find so much as a broken tree branch. The steady drizzle washed away our clumsy footsteps. Any traces of Jimmy were gone. Finding him would come as a surprise for whoever tripped over him.

The carcass of what I thought to be a bunny washed down past my feet. I screeched, not a full-fledged scream, more of a girly "eeak." The somber mood of the group kept Ross and Harvey from teasing me about my reaction. After six hours of yelling and slogging through the mire, I was all Jimmy-ed out. Ross called an early end to the search when lightening filled the horizon. I took my pointy hat off.

Hey, if Jimmy can see me in a purple, pointy hat with sunflowers, so can Thor.

The team got even smaller on the third day. The regulars had jobs they returned to, including Harv. Claire went back to work at the B & G, but she sent a cooler of drinks with us and offered dinner when we finished searching for the day. Dr. Word at the vet clinic accepted my absence without argument. Spring births would start in a couple of weeks, but we were in a slow patch of our year.

Deputy Ron manned the Sheriff's office. David Blue Sky and Jason brought two horses to compensate for the lack of manpower, and the rougher terrain we expected to cover. We walked a grid of land higher up than we'd been the first two days. The footpaths and deer trails disappeared. The denser forest and lack of sunlight lent a sinister feel to our surroundings.

The old song "Little Red Riding Hood," kept playing in my mind, over and over. Only the words changed to, "Hey there Little Purple Pointy Hat. I know exactly where you're at, and you're everything that a big bad wolf could want." I tried not to hum the melody. I considered it an act of kindness not to stick the song in anyone else's head.

It beats listening to an elevator "muzak" rendition of Mozart's "Prayer for the Dead," also available on my private channel.

Ross and David rode ahead. Jason and five of us scoured thickets, underbrush, and the wooded boles we hadn't reached on Sunday. We'd been out forty-five minutes.

"Jimmy!" My voice sounded hoarse from calling out as we walked. Everything hurt. I sucked in a breath to shout his name again and gagged. "Jason, we need to stop the line," I said.

"What's up Nan?" Jason asked.

How do I tell him this phlegmy, sweet-sour taste in the back of my throat means I've found Jimmy?

I must have paled enough to worry him because Jason called to the others. "Oi, bring it to a stop and take a load off!"

"Oi?" English street slang seemed incongruous with Jason's shoulder length black hair and striking American Indian features. It threw me for a moment. "Oi?" I repeated and giggled. It came out with a hint of hysteria.

"G-paw and I watch a lot of British TV." Jason shrugged, "I like the sound of it."

"Me too." I wiped my eyes, but they were leaking faster than my sleeves could dry. "You should talk to my housemate. He has a whole list of BBC favorites."

"The big man likes Brit TV? That surprises me," said Jason.

Oh God, I really, really don't want to pass out in front of these people.

I swayed, and Jason reached to steady me.

"Please walky-talky your G-paw and Ross. Tell them I

taste Jimmy."

Jason gave me an incredulous stare.

"They'll understand what I mean." I grabbed for my flask and gargled. I spit the rancid tasting vodka out of my mouth, but the taste of death remained.

David and Ross arrived in about five minutes. The horses weren't lathered, but they were sweaty. The guys had ridden the painted ponies as fast as their old riders could go.

Ross jumped down and ran to me. "Are you alright?" He grabbed me by the shoulders and shook me.

"Don't mind him. He's cranky because he's got a blister on his butt," explained David.

"I've got a saddle sore from riding your ornery, old gelding. He found every gopher hole and empty rabbit warren along ten miles of fencing," snapped Ross as he let go of me. He was breathing fast.

I glared at Jason and asked him, "What did you say to them?"

"Sorry, Nan. I thought you were going all Dr. Who on me," Jason apologized.

"What's on second?" I asked.

My Abbott and Costello reference got lost on him. I couldn't be mad. Not many people got my humor. Jason hadn't been around me much. All he knew were rumors the townsfolk told. From the look on everyone's face, I was no longer one cat short of crazy. Fifteen seemed to be the magic number that flipped me from she likes cats, skipped over the excuse of becoming a nonprofit shelter, and dumped me right on the doorstep of daffy-doodles.

Good to know.

"I'm fine," I announced to the general public. I wanted to add "not insane," but I refrained. This wasn't about me. I rubbed my forehead trying to keep the headache from encroaching. I told Ross and David, "Jimmy's near. I can't see him, but I can . . ." I swallowed with difficulty.

Ross put his hand on my shoulder and gave me a comforting squeeze.

Time to put on my big girl panties and spit it out.

"I can taste him, Ross, in the back of my throat. He's close."

Tears rolled down my face. David hopped down from his horse with a spryness that belied his age. He handed the reins to Jason. The elder Blue Sky lifted his face to the heavens and sniffed the air. He pointed to a clutter of ash trees we hadn't walked through yet.

"You stay here," Ross ordered me. "Three days gone in

the woods, in this weather, is not pretty."

"Three weeks in a condo is not great either," I muttered under my breath.

Ross hugged me. "You don't need to see this." He turned to the group. "Jason, you stay with Nan and the horses. George, Cody, you come with David and me. Everyone else please remain here for a few minutes while we check this out. Mooch, stay." There was no mistaking his commands or the concern in his voice.

Cody had been an army war correspondent in Iraq. He moved to Angel Falls with his family after an IED took the lower part of his left leg. Cody embraced the mantle of the unofficial town morgue/crime scene photographer. He shot pictures of Breaking-and-Entering aftermaths, the occasional Grand Theft Auto parts left behind, and the new artwork created by local taggers (both of them). Not much spooked Cody, except Halloween at my house. He let his daughter Trick or Treat with us, but he never took pictures at Seven Hilltop Street. "Too spooky," he told Claire.

Cody pulled a camera out of his backpack and followed David and George.

I'd met George, but didn't know much about him. He drank beer at Claire's now and again on my Friday nights, and shot some Eight Ball. He didn't talk much, never bet on the outcome of the pool tables, and always left after three beers . . . no matter how long it took him to drink them.

Ross tried to be subtle when he grabbed his backpack off the horse. Jason and I knew a body bag lay folded inside it. We watched from a distance as camera flashes shot through the air. The bright yellow crime scene tape came out. David wove it through the trees like a strangle vine.

Half an hour later four serious, strong men carried a black bag toward those of us who waited. It looked small in their hands. Tears welled in Cody's eyes. Ross's nose ran and he wiped it with his sleeve. Stoic sorrow made David and George look like walking statues. Jason rushed to get the collapsible gurney from the horse packs. His grandfather waved him off with a subtle hand gesture. They would carry Jimmy down to town by hand. Reality hit. All our hats came off, and we fell into a different kind of line behind the four pallbearers.

I reached for my vodka flask and finished it.

Grave Intentions

Ross sent Jimmy's remains to the Medical Examiner's office in Zoerne. Pronounced "Sorn" not "Zoor Knee." Zoerne, the next town over, was located north of Angel Falls. They had a mall, a Bennigan's, a DSW (Designer Shoe Warehouse), a multi-plex movie theatre, and a lot of other amenities that we did not have in our little burg. Angel Falls was not big enough to have a forensic department of its own or a police department. We did have a medi-clinic, a medi-spa, a midwife, three privately practicing physicians, one dentist, one lawyer, and a group of volunteer firefighters.

Ross avoided me for several days and kept a tight lip about the entire Jimmy incident. I think he got scolded for moving Jimmy without an official coroner pronouncing at the site. In direct contrast, the rest of our community buzzed with rumor and speculation. Friday night Claire's Bar and Grill filled to capacity and flowed out onto the picnic tables out back. Normally, that kind of crowd didn't happen until Memorial Day. Everyone wanted to know what was "really going on."

My usual forty-five minute Tarot card readings changed to fifteen minutes for twenty bucks with the caveat that the customer's final question could have nothing to do with Jimmy's death. Claire hid the bottle of Crown after the first hour and started me on beer. The Bar and Grill was not a smoke-free zone. The Angel Falls town council hadn't passed the proper ordinances to forbid public smoking, yet. Tobacco haze hung low and mixed with the smell of overused cooking oil from all the curly fries JD cooked up for the hungry group.

I'd never been a part of a flash mob, or fan-boy riot. I imagined tonight's gathering being similar to those that came to view a hanging or beheading. The people here were at once horrified, and yet somehow exhilarated by Jimmy's death. Add in a few beers and the speculation and gossip grew.

The noise level seemed exponentially louder than normal, and my head throbbed over my right eye. Pool balls clacked against each other, sounding like symbols crashing in my ears. Several times during the night a toast went up to Jimmy's memory. When Claire rang the ship's bell for "Last Call," Laura waved her cleaning cloth like a victory towel. Or was it a white flag of surrender?

"Whew!" she exclaimed, "Made it through the rough waters."

I breathed a sigh of relief, too. The final patron of the night paid his tab, tipped his hat to the ladies, and left. Ross came into the bar and locked the door behind him.

"What are you doing out this late?" I asked him.

Claire interrupted, "Sheriff, I got a draft beer in glass. I'm going to pour it out if you don't drink it."

"Much obliged," answered Ross.

Claire nodded to Laura. Her niece filled a beer mug for my cousin. Ross strolled over beside me, and sipped his brew while I stuffed my psychic paraphernalia into my bag: candle, crystal ball, ceramic dragon, and Tarot cards.

"Sit," I invited.

He did. His reddish-brown hair twinkled with grey highlights like mine. He was only six months older than me. His chiseled features placed him on a line between handsome for his age and just plain pretty. I'd never say that to his face; he'd punch me out of embarrassment. His shirt and blue jeans were starched and pressed, his gig line straight. He embodied courage, intelligence and kindness. I liked him. He was one of the good-guys, even wore a white hat. Okay, light beige.

Naomi Patterson

I looked at my watch, Doc's old stainless steel Rolex. I no longer wore it out of sentiment; I wore it because the face was large enough for me to read without contacts or glasses.

"You're out late. Where's that lovely wife of yours this evening?" I asked and added, "Or should I say this morning?"

"Church lock-in with the kids. They're watching a movie and camping out in the sanctuary," he said.

"You got guards posted?" I asked half-joking.

I took my purple hat off and grimaced at the sunflowers. I hadn't bothered with my box o' hair tonight. I had barely managed eyeliner and lipstick. I sported my own long, calico tresses with apathy.

Ross crossed his hands in front of his eyes like I was too scary to bear. "Fix your hair, Nannie. You look like Medusa, an old, tired Medusa."

I stuck my tongue out at him and pulled my hair back into a ponytail, so I wouldn't give him a heart attack. Once my locks were controlled, he peeked through his fingers at me and answered my question about guards at the church.

"A few fathers with Concealed Carry Permits are walking the perimeter." He paused. "What made you ask that?"

"Something feels off." I made my eyes bug out and cackled. "Dare I say odd?"

"How much have you had to drink?" He sputtered and wiped his mouth.

"Well, officer, it was a busy night. I didn't have time to drink, much. I'm not driving, if that's what you are worried about."

"Yeah, well you're not walking home alone either." Ross raised his voice. "I'll have another, Miss Claire, if you let me pay for it."

"Register's closed," hollered Claire, as she helped JD clean up the kitchen.

Less than two minutes later, two sandwiches and two more beers appeared at our table. Laura hugged me goodnight.

"Aunt Claire says to turn the lights out, and lock the back door when you leave."

"Will do. Thanks for managing the crowd tonight," I said.

"No problem, Nan. I'm sorry Jimmy's dead, but I made more in tips this week than I did all last month. Death is good for business." Laura blushed. "I didn't mean for it to come out that way."

"You didn't intend any harm to Jimmy by saying it. I know that," I comforted her with a pat on her hands.

"How are you getting home, Laura?" Ross asked.

"My boyfriend's waiting outside in his pickup, and we're going straight home. I promise," she answered.

"That boy treating you right?" Ross raised a fatherly eyebrow.

"Yes, sir."

Ross waved her on her way. I swear she curtsied to him. The bar back fell into darkness. I hadn't noticed when Claire and JD left. They felt odd, too. The kitchen had been noisy tonight, pans being banged, plates being tossed, not placed in the sink. Maybe the frenzy of the packed house overwhelmed them, but I suspected an underlying argument caused the ruckus. I bit into my BLT. I hadn't realized how hungry I was. Ross and I scarfed our sandwiches.

"How come I get this late-night dinner date?" I asked.

Ross wiped some mayo from the corner of his mouth before answering. "Nan, are you missing any cats at home? Or at the clinic?"

"We've got Miss Sue's fat tabby in the clinic. At home we don't do a head count every night, but I don't think so." I belched with gusto. "Why?"

"Nice one!" he acknowledged.

"Challenge?"

He tried to burp, but couldn't bring himself to such bad

manners.

"Ha, ha, ha, ha, ha, ha. I win!" I tormented. "Why missing cats?"

"No reason."

"You are such a liar!"

My cousin did not lie. He was, however, skilled in withholding information. Ross had a stone-cold poker face when he wanted, but I knew him. The vein on his forehead over his left eye pulsed with his heart.

"Fine. You don't have to say anything." I wiped bacon grease off my fingers and reached back in my bag for my cards. "I have my ways."

"Don't," he said, his voice just short of a command.

"I don't like that tone of voice." I continued to shuffle my dragons.

"Nan, don't," he repeated and added, "Please."

"Then talk to me, Cuz," I suggested, and put the cards down.

"I had a bad dream," he admitted. "I saw Harvey washing blood off your hands."

"And?" I wiped my hands on my skirt.

Ross finished his beer. "I got a piece of information from the medical examiner in Zoerne. I'm not sure how to process it."

121

"About Jimmy?" I asked. "Tell."

"I'm not sure I can," he answered. "It's part of an on-going investigation. I'm not supposed to discuss it with civilians."

"Oh, please," I interrupted. I did the two-fingered, eye-to-eye, I-see-you motion twice. "It's late. I'm not in the mood to play twenty questions with you, and then have to try and figure out what I'm suppose to understand by what you don't say."

"The ME doing the autopsy found some foreign matter in Jimmy's remains, in his throat. He called me and wanted me to email the crime scene photos."

"Crime scene? It might be an accident scene."

"Not so much, Cuz. Jimmy was strangled, his neck broken in the attack, and the examiner found a piece of cat intestine."

I felt beer, bacon and bile rising in my throat. "Someone strangled him with catgut? Are you serious?"

"The lab we sent Jimmy's remains to isn't high tech. The lab ghouls do their best with what they have," Ross explained. "Their not sure. They found a line, a string, call it what you will, a piece of cat intestine in his neck area."

"But he could have fallen, landed funny," I struggled for any explanation other than murder.

"Yeah, he could have," my cousin conceded to placate me. "He could have been walking miles from his home, all alone, at midnight, in the rain, stumbled, fallen, on his way down wrapped the innards of a dead cat around his throat, and then for good measure landed so as to snap his own neck."

"When you put it that way," I smacked him on the shoulder.

"Left on our own in nature, with wild animals and wet weather we," he struggled to find the correct words.

"We get mushy," I suggested.

"Rather quickly. The integrity of forensic evidence doesn't last forever. Nan, we may never know the truth about what happened to Jimmy."

My thoughts went to Doc. He told me he needed to be alone for a while to figure out what he wanted for the rest of his life. I didn't understand what he wanted was to die. I went on vacation expecting everything to be back to normal when I came home. It wasn't. I wasn't. Nothing would ever be normal for me, ever again. I stared into the darkest corner of the Bar and Grill.

I need something stronger than beer.

"I'm sorry, Nan. I didn't think about how all this would affect you. Stupid of me." Ross brought a bottle of Southern Comfort from behind the bar over to our table and poured me a shot.

I patted his hand affectionately and waved him off. Like Harvey, Ross was one of my champions, and I loved him beyond words.

"Death by Catgut. Great line for the Chamber of Commerce tourism brochures," I mumbled. Angel Falls didn't have a Chamber of Commerce. "Another example of how Incubus Falls sucks the life out of its residences."

"That's dark. From Angel to Incubus?" he questioned.

"I'm dark," I admitted.

I kicked back a second jigger then got up to clean our plates and glasses. Ross followed me into the kitchen. Ross moved like his lower back hurt from too much time on horseback. I wondered if he'd been back in the woods hunting for bad guys. I caught our reflections in the glass cabinet doors. Our ethereal forms floated against the stainless steel background.

How did we get to this moment, standing in the dark with soapy hands and sad faces?

"Step-by-step," Ross whispered as though he had heard my thoughts. He cleared his throat. "Nan, not many people can list the multi-purposes of catgut."

"Let's see: violin strings, sutures, sausage . . . early

tennis rackets," I speculated. "If you cure the gut, it can be braided into jewelry like elephant hair bracelets, only more disgusting. Wait, harp strings, maybe. I'm not really versed on musical instrument construction. I assume we've modern substitutions."

Ross nodded in agreement. "You're missing the point, Nan."

"Enlighten me."

Ross dried the dishes as I washed. "Look, we don't know if Jimmy was strangled with catgut, or if it was a coyote with bad flossing issues." He chomped his teeth.

I raised my hands into the time-out signal they used in football. "I change my mind. Over-sharing, Cuz."

"The point is, if I were putting together a Murder Book, and I may have to, the top three 'people of interest' would be Claire, Harvey and *you*."

"Oh."

Suspects

Not being sure how a suspect acted, the next morning I set about my daily routine. This Saturday I had duties at the vet clinic. We had two overnight guests that needed my attention. Doogie Doggie was an elderly beagle sequestered in our kennel for biting at his ingrown toenail. When not enjoying our hospitality, Doogie lived with his littermate, Ima Doggie. Sometimes pet owner humor escaped me.

Of course, I have a cat named Phizner Pinash Scagmite the Cute. Who am I to cast stones?

Feisty, the obese tabby I told Ross about was in our care due to a neck abscess. Both dog and cat were confined. They wore an ElizaSoft collar, a.k.a. "the cone of shame" to keep them from chewing or scratching at their wounds. For a brief second, I imagined myself in a huge blue plastic collar bumping into walls.

Shame on me, trying to chew out my own heart.

I dismissed the vision and walked Doogie outside for a potty break. When the beasties were fed and properly played with, I locked them up and promised them that Dr. Word would come in later to check on their progress and take them to their families, if they were ready to go.

Dr. Word was a hands-on veterinarian. She had five dogs of her own and a pot-belly pig that she described as a wirehair terrier with a cloven hoof disorder. I enjoyed being around her.

Work done, I wanted to go to the B & G, but it was too early. I wound my way through the pecan trees that line the main street. My steps listed to the left tugging me in the direction of the Bar and Grill in spite of my good intentions to pass it by. I knew where Claire kept the spare key. When I got inside, I discovered Claire sitting alone, in the morning dark. Her eyes were closed. I thought she might be sleeping, but she waved at me when I walked further in.

"Whatcha doing?" I asked.

She raised her empty glass of Crown Royal. "Having breakfast."

"Breakfast of champions?"

"You hungry? We'll need another bottle of instant breakfast."

"Sure. I think I'll have mine with orange juice and

pretend it's healthy."

"You know where the bar is."

I slid behind the counter and opened the mini-fridge to grab some juice.

"Got your cards with you? I need a reading," Claire slurred.

"I ran by the clinic. I didn't even bring my wallet. You're here early?"

"Yeah," she mumbled.

It had been a while for her, but I recognized that look. "How long have you been here?" I waltzed in her direction with an invisible partner.

"Since about five o'clock this morning."

"Yes. And, how long you been drinking?" I asked.

"Since about five o'clock this morning."

On cue we both sang the refrain to the old Alan Jackson/Jimmy Buffet song, "It's five o'clock somewhere."

I didn't need my Tarot cards to figure this out. "JD?"

"Yup."

"You have a fight?"

"He left."

"Why?" When she didn't answer I continued, "Hey, I'll give you something else to brood over. You were right, I am a suspect in Jimmy's disappearance. Well, now it's his murder. So is Harvey. Isn't that interesting?" I didn't mention her in the list. She had enough on her mind.

"Murder? Murder! That's not funny, Nan." Claire lit another cigarette.

"Didn't mean it to be. That's why Ross came by last night."

"Shit. Shit, shit, shittity, shit, shit." Claire got up and did her version of River Dance. "That means JD and me are suspects, too."

"Actually, it's 'Persons of Interest'," I corrected her. "Yes, it looks that way."

Claire hiccupped. She ran her tongue across her teeth. "Yew. My choppers are fuzzy."

"You go brush your teeth, and I'll make a pot of coffee," I suggested.

"Coffee. Nannie, you're being mean," she said as she walked toward the wench's room. "Nobody likes a wide-awake drunk."

When she emerged her face had been washed and her hair brushed as well as her teeth. Not much she could do about her rumpled clothes. She flashed her clean smile at me. I poured us each a cup of Jamaican java and passed her a piece of toast.

She reached across me and grabbed a brandy bottle. More than a jigger went into her coffee. I pulled the bottle away from her and splashed a few polite drops into my cup.

Friends don't let friends drink alone this early in the day.

"Spill it," I demanded.

She blew air through her lips and made them raspberry. "In no particular order the answers are: The town is getting too noisy, I'm getting too nosey, I was the second-to-the-last person to see Jimmy alive, and JD wasn't home the night Jimmy went missing."

"And the questions are?" I hummed the theme song to *Jeopardy.*

"Why did JD leave? Why am I a suspect? And last but not least, why is JD a suspect?" Claire bowed her head to me and changed the words to "a person of interest."

"The night Jimmy went missing? JD left for home at ten when Laura did. You and I stayed here with Jimmy waiting for the storm that never came, and we all left together," I stated.

"Not exactly." She reached for another piece of toast. "Since it wasn't raining that hard, I decided to come back and get Mutt. Jimmy came bursting in a few moments later and mumbled something about forgetting his hat."

130

Death By Catgut

"I don't remember him wearing a hat," I said.

"That's cause his daddy raised him right. He takes his hat off inside."

"Okay."

"No, not okay. Jimmy was upset, agitated, fidgety," Claire explained.

"Jimmy is always jittery." I couldn't refer to him in the past tense. "And I fainted. He was concerned."

"I'll admit you sprawled on my floor was a scary sight for those who have never seen such a thing before." She grinned lopsided. "But Jimmy behaved oddly. I mean more than his everyday two steps to the left of center. I didn't pay attention. I wanted to go home. When I got to the house, JD wasn't there. Again, I didn't pay attention. I went to bed. I did notice JD's boots were muddy and wet the next morning when I got up, and Mutt hadn't been taken on his breakfast walk." She stirred her coffee with her finger. "So, that's my story. What's yours? The reason your cousin has you in his crosshairs would be?"

Maybe if I say it fast it won't sound crazy. What the hell?

"I work in a veterinarian clinic, and apparently have access to all kinds of animal pieces and parts. I live with a taxidermist and fifteen cats, not counting Stanley and Sienna, who are stuffed. I know many uses for intestines other than food processing, and Ross says that the ME thinks Jimmy may have been strangled to death with catgut."

Claire started laughing. She laughed until she fell off the barstool. I raced around the counter to help her.

"Are you all right?" I blurted.

She farted and continued to giggle. "Excuse me. Garroted by el gato. Sounds like the plot of a bad TV novella. Now, that's funny."

"What's funny?"

"You, me, Harvey-the-boy-scout, suspects in a murder?" Claire continued to giggle.

"I found Jimmy," I defended my right to be a person of interest.

"You smelled him," she accused with a snicker.

"I tasted him," I corrected.

"That is gross. I don't even want to think about that. And, I don't want to think about why JD begged out of the search with," she made quote signs with her fingers, "a 'backache.' That man was strong enough to lift half a cow into the freezer."

"You keep half a cow in the freezer?"

"No, Nan. You know what I mean. He left too quickly after we found Jimmy's body."

"Aren't you over-reacting? I mean neither of us has a good track record in the 'happily ever after' department, but do you really think you've been sleeping with a killer?"

I pulled her up from the floor, rocked back on my heels in an overcompensation to jerk her up. We both fell kit-over-caboodle and landed on our rumps. When the laughter subsided, Claire glanced at the portrait of herself above the bar. A surrealistic painting, it portrayed Captain Claire at the helm of a two-masted schooner in the high seas off of Barbados.

Well, one and a half masts . . . it's a fantasy stormscape.

"I've known worse," she admitted.

I went for the wide-eyed surprised look.

"Pirates," she stated flatly. "Damn pirates. They always go for the heart."

I couldn't tell if Claire was serious or playing.

"Did you see Harvey when you got home that night?" she asked as we grappled each other to stand up.

"Yeah."

"What time?"

"After midnight, before dawn."

"Girlfriend, none of us has an alibi. Repeat after me, Al-Li-Bi. Anybody's capable of homicide, suicide, any kind of 'cide' the human condition can concoct. Say that three times real fast . . . condition-can-concoct, condition-can-concoct, condition-can-concoct. In the eyes of the law any one of us could have killed Jimmy. You have any attorneys on speed dial?" asked Claire.

"I don't have a cell phone."

"How do you exist in this world?"

"We've got the one lawyer here in town. I don't remember his name. Do you?"

She shook her head, "He's not a drinking man or a pool player. I don't think he's ever been in here."

"Could he represent all of us?"

"He may have to," Claire said. "I'm going home. I need some Tylenol. I feel a heartache coming on." She pressed her knuckles into her chest as if that would help ease the pain.

"Do you want to come to my house? You won't have to be around all of JD's stuff," I offered. "Maybe you shouldn't be alone."

"Thanks, but no thanks. The old jarhead left taking all that he came with, an olive green duffel bag and a smile. Besides, Mutt needs me. That dog's going to miss JD something awful. They took their morning walks together. Slow and easy." Claire wiped tears from her check. "The 'Gone Fishing' sign's beside the door. Will you prop it in the window? I don't have a cook, and I don't feel like sharing my booze."

"You want Harv and me to help out? We could open tonight with Laura. Maybe drinks and peanuts only?"

"Ask me again later. I need to sleep through some of this loss." She waved goodbye.

I was reluctant to let her go. "Hey, do you want to have a memorial service for Jimmy? I think his cousin, Joe, is Jimmy's next of kin, but he may not know how to handle the situation."

Claire stopped in the doorway. The inside shadows fell across her face and the morning sun backlit her body. She floated there like a mermaid between swells.

"Do you think huddling together with a drink in our hands will make the pain go away?" she asked me in a little girl voice.

I knew she needed comfort, reassurance, but she also wanted the truth. She wasn't asking about the memorial service.

"No," I answered her. "But I keep trying. You want me to walk you home?"

Claire shook her head and left without saying anything more.

I turned the coffee pot off; wishing the pain of the latest season of my life could be switched off as easily. "Find your happy place, Nannie," I told myself. I raised my arms above my head and did a tippy-toe ballet across a few planks of pine floor. Long ago, in a place far away, dancing made me smile. Unsteady in flip-flops, I kicked them off, and swung into a pirouette.

Hot damn. I can still spin with the best of them.

I spiraled again, putting effort into it this time and arrived at the door a moment before the sadness caught up with me. I hung the "Gone Fishing" plaque up on the door and marched my tutu home.

Death By Catgut

A Dirt Nap

Like some injured animals, Claire went to ground when she needed to heal. I let her be with the understanding that if she hid longer than a week, I'd seek her out. She emerged from her emotional chrysalis four days later, no worse for her worries. I was her opposite when I got upset, nervous energy came to me instead of sleep. In an effort to do a controlled release rather than my usual version of a manic chipmunk, I decided to dig in the dirt. The activity brought me a certain peace of mind. I kept my herb garden year-round, and Harvey plowed up a small plot for vegetables on our back lot each spring and fall. I hadn't even decided what veggies to plant this season.

I spaded a patch of ground under our kitchen window. Forget-Me-Nots longed to grow in this flowerbed with a sprinkling of guardian Snapdragons mixed in and Coxcomb as border. Mama made a garden no matter where we were stationed. Sometimes she sufficed with window boxes other times she glorified our entire backyards. I inherited the need to stick my fingers in the dirt. Snowball, Cricket, and Phizner consulted with me on my home improvement efforts, but I lost one of my helpers when Phizner became distracted by a pill bug.

A few things were bugging me this morning, too. I wondered if Claire had been sharing her bed with a murderer all winter; if my cousin, the sheriff, believed Harvey and I were capable of committing such a gruesome act as strangling Jimmy to death by catgut; if a stranger passing through Angel Falls had infiltrated our little community and perpetrated such a crime, unseen and unknown; or worst of all, if someone I'd known all my life, snapped over the price of Premium Unleaded and killed Jimmy in protest.

Phizner brought me his saliva-covered prize. I sat down to say thank you and scratched his neck. I got easily distracted, too.

Through the open window above my head, I heard Claire and Harvey amble into the kitchen. The old plank floor squeaked and grocery bags crinkled on the countertop. I wasn't hiding from them, merely out of their line of sight. I grabbed my hand trowel and kept jabbing at the indifferent soil. They were in the middle of what sounded like a long conversation.

"It's time for her to get on with her life," Harvey stated emphatically. "Hey, I liked the guy. And for a time, Doc was good for Nan. But, this 'shame and blame' shit has got to stop. He's dead. He's been dead a long time. Nan needs to move on!" Harvey's voice had an annoyed edge to it.

"Are you really that heartless?" asked Claire.

"If wanting her to join us in the land of the living is heartless, then I am. The whole purpose of the grieving process is to acknowledge the loss, allow us time to adjust to the loss, and then to come back from the loss, to our lives. Different for the sorrow, yes, but able to cope. It's been five years, and Nan's still an emotional zombie."

"That's kind of harsh, big guy."

"Really? So, these nose-dives she's been taking are fine by you?"

"No, Harv. They are not."

"Look, I understand we see things differently. I'm a guy . . ."

"Oh, honey, you are indeed!"

I heard my best friend flirting with my best housemate.

"Claire, stop it. I'm angry. I've been on two suicide watches for Nan. So have you. One after Doc left her to figure out his life, and one after she found out he cheated on her. I'm not thrilled with the prospect of a third."

"Fine. Your point would be?" Claire asked.

Harvey sighed. "Guys will say anything, but it's what we do that matters."

Claire was chain-smoking which let me know she felt anxious about me too. I smelled singed tobacco through the open window. Normally, she didn't light up anywhere except the Bar and Grill.

I didn't mean to hurt them like this. I'd kept them trapped with me in my infinite loop of sorrow. If she and Harv had been talking about the weather, I'd have stood up, scared the hell out of them, and enjoyed the fun of startling them. Their conversation had grown too personal for me to pop up and announce I'd been eavesdropping. I felt guilty enough for putting them through yet another death anniversary.

"And?" Claire prompted.

"Doc left everything to Nan, *everything*. That is not the action of a man planning to spend the rest of his life in the arms of another woman, no matter what kind of guilt or obligation he feels. Doc contacted his broker and his lawyer only a couple of months before he died to reaffirm his wishes that Nan be his sole beneficiary."

"I didn't know that," Claire admitted.

"And three weeks before he killed himself Nan asked Doc to remove her from his estate. He sent her a one word email . . . 'NO'."

"You read her email?"

"At that point in Nan's life, you bet your ass. Do you not remember what it was like trying to keep her alive after Doc left her?"

"I remember." Claire sounded petulant.

"I don't understand why he did what he did. But maybe he did her a favor," Harvey defended his position.

"Excuse me, did I hear you correctly?"

"If Nan hadn't found out about the affair, Doc would have remained Prince Charming forever: the perfect man, tormented by his inner demons, dancing into death to escape the pain of . . . breathing. Melody was nothing more than his escape hatch -- a five-fuck fantasy and fare-thee-well."

"Cleaver. Are you trying out for poet laureate of Angel Falls?"

Harvey slammed his fist down on the countertop.

"If Nan had known Doc planned to kill himself she would have stopped him, or we'd have buried them both. Melody, on the other hand, got out while the getting was good. Doc knew both of his women. He knew Nan would go down with him if he let her, and he knew Mel would dump his ass so he would have an excuse to kill himself."

"Don't be theatrical, sweetie," admonished Claire.

"Sure thing, *sweetie*, but you do the comparison. An obsessive-compulsive man like Doc living with his sins intact and on display for everyone he cared about to see, or dying with his iniquities hidden away. Which one would you pick?"

"I'm standing here aren't I?" Claire said.

I heard Claire pop the cork on a wine bottle and pour. I wanted to inhale the heady woodiness of the Merlot I had left on the kitchen counter, but beyond the smoke from her cigarette only mulch and cat poop reached my nostrils.

"Outside of some nasty emails, some late night phone conversations, probably after her husband went to sleep, and a few cross country booty-calls, this Melody person got a lousy deal. Doc told his old college fuck-buddy one thing and Nan another." Harvey admitted, "I read Doc and Melody's emails too. Come-on, thirteen-year olds couldn't be more melodramatic. I'm surprised they didn't design avatars for themselves. It was RPG in the highest."

"Let me get this straight. Your explanation for Doc almost destroying our best friend's spirit is a fantasy vacation into Betrayal Land?" asked Claire.

"No. Look, nothing can change what went down, good-bad, right-wrong. That's my point. It's done. I am tired of this conversation, year after year," he stated flatly.

"Oh, poor Doc, torn between two lovers. Role Playing Games, my ass."

"Have you never been in love with two people at the same time?"

"Hell no!" she spat. "I'm a serial monogamist."

"Lucky you," Harvey whispered.

My heart tried to claw its way out of my chest. I prayed Claire and Harvey wouldn't hear it pounding. I needed to focus on something, anything other than the pain. My favorite memories of Doc were not his grandiose gestures – the jewelry and vacations. Instead, they were small moments between us: dancing in the kitchen while we cooked dinner, snuggling by the fire while we watched TV, chasing each other around the backyard to steal a kiss, laughing while we made love. Why wasn't that enough for him?

Why wasn't I enough?

Claire must have tapped her smoldering tobacco out on the bottom of her sandal because singed shoe leather wafted into my nose along with her menthol cigarettes. Max found me. He head-butted my thigh then chirruped for more of our Hilltop clan to rally around. Sammie, Cedric and Toby came running and snuggled in close to me. My furry earth angels kept me from breaking into tiny pieces and crumbling into the flowerbed beneath me.

"Doc screwed up, but in the end where was his loyalty?" Harvey challenged her.

"Leaving Nan a broken-down condo and a bank account doesn't make up for what he did," sneered Claire as she defended my broken heart. "All his honor and promises came to nothing."

Nothing? No one's life should come to nothing. Oh Doc, have I used up all our love in sorrow?

"You're right. The last couple of years he turned into a shit-bag, and if I'd known what was going down, he and I would have had more than words," Harvey declared. "But here's something else to think about. How pathetic is it if the greatest love of Nan's life stays the guy who broke her? Doesn't she deserve better?"

Pathetic. Love of my life. Broken.

I took my gardening gloves off and stared at Doc and my promise rings. I pulled them off my hand and buried them in the flowerbed. Tux dug them back up, so I put them back on, dirt and all.

Death By Catgut

"This stuff with Jimmy brought up issues for all of us, but more for Nan. It's like she's being punished for not knowing how to stop eventuality." Claire sniffed, and continued in a softer voice, "What if Nan decides its time for her to go find Doc on the other side? That veil between life and death is thinner for her than the rest of us. She could step over that invisible line, and we'd lose her. We could lose her, Harvey. There's something different about her this year. I'm scared."

Harvey's heavy footsteps crossed over to where Claire stood. Although he whispered, I heard him. "Yeah, me too."

I lay down in the dirt. *Me three.*

When they left the kitchen I got up and brushed the grime off. I could feel the garden hose impression on my cheek from where I had laid my head. If I had to deal with more dying, I needed more beer. I kept a small refrigerator out in the greenhouse stocked with Lone Star Longnecks for such emergencies.

There were several pictures in magnetic frames clinging to the side of the fridge. Faded from sunlight and age, one picture was from a family fishing trip. The photo included our dog and Harvey. I had never noticed before, except for the age difference they looked alike. Their faces and noses were the same shape, Harvey and my brother Zach, not Harvey and the dog.

Ahh, Stripe.

A week before my father killed himself, Zach, my closest brother in age and mindset, had to put his dog down. Stripe was our eleven-year old Dalmatian. She hurt with arthritis and failing kidneys. Back then we had no access to merciful, pink fluid administered by kindly doctors. There was only our father's .38 caliber revolver and his admonishment: "Don't let the dog suffer, Son. And, don't waste any bullets."

Zach said he'd take her into the woods. I asked if I could go along.

"Nah, just me and her today," he said. "Walk, girl?"

Stripe did her best to perk up. I couldn't understand why Zach took a shovel and a blanket with him. They were gone all afternoon. I remembered the look in my brother's eyes when he returned home alone.

"Where's Stripe?" I'd asked, not comprehending the magnitude of their journey.

"She's taking a dirt nap, Nannie."

"But she'll get cold lying on the ground!"

"I covered her up with the blanket from my bed."

Zach hadn't finished crying over Stripe by the time we buried Daddy. To this day, I didn't know whom he mourned for more, our dog or our father.

Six months after Daddy, Granny Winnie died from a stress-induced heart attack. My father had been her only son. When he died she gave up. Her passing completed my first set of "Death Threes," but it wasn't my last.

Half a six-pack of memories later I came back to myself. Jimmy's murder began another round of threes. My whole body shook. I worried for who would be the next two deaths on the Reaper's list. Time for bed, if only I could sleep. Punkin came into the greenhouse to guide me toward the house. My pretty orange soul mate knew when to come get me. I picked her up to carry her in.

"Thank you," I nuzzled into her silky neck ruff.

Claire and Mutt were long gone. I assumed Harvey slept. I could hear several of our kitties snoring on the sofa.

Damn, not sleepy.

I grabbed my dragon deck of cards from the bookshelf and plopped down next to sleeping cats. Dilapidated and threadbare, the couch felt more comfortable than the lawn chair in the greenhouse. I had difficulty reading my own future. I thought of Harvey and Claire while I shuffled. I noticed Claire spending more time here since JD's sudden exit. She reopened the bar and grill, but only served drinks.

I pulled out my comfort cards and stroked the dragons on the back cover of the top card. I laid out the Celtic Cross to see what the future would bring them. Another couple of beers, and maybe the dragons would sing for me like they did for Granny Winnie.

Death By Catgut

It Comes in Threes

The next morning Harvey came home with a road-kill cat-in-the-bag. There wasn't a lot of blood. The stray died from the blunt force impact without getting gushy on the outside.

My housemate was not in the habit of picking dead things up off the road. My wicked side kicked in. "Breakfast?" I made my goofy face.

"Tastes like chicken to me."

"Ugh, you win. Coffee instead."

"Yes, please."

Harv had confusing ethics when it came to our furry children bearing witness to his hobby. Animals understood death, not necessarily desertion. Whenever one of our pets crossed-over to chase butterflies on the other side we had a "viewing" for our four-footed housemates to sniff and say goodbye. The cat in Harv's arms didn't come from our colony, so it posed no emotional threat to our beastie-babies. Nonetheless, he had the carcass wrapped in plastic and picked up his pace through the second floor as he headed for his inner sanctum on level three. The cats were not allowed up there, too many chemicals and sharp objects. I left a game of tickle-toes with Ashley and Merlin to follow Harv up the rickety stairs.

His studio didn't look like a horror movie version of the mad re-animator. He did have test tubes and a microscope. He also had sketchbooks and a several animal gross anatomy tomes. Harvey kept his workspace clean and smelling as nice as an area dedicated to dead animals could. He had a legitimate necropsy table, the kind vets use, complete with surgical lighting, an overhead rinsing apparatus and drain system. The body fluids and small miscellaneous parts from his work went into the garden for fertilizer. When our zoo was open, healthy body parts went to help feed the carnivores, now the leftovers went to the animal crematorium.

Harvey always respected his clients. He pulled the once pretty cat out of the plastic shroud, and gently placed its floppy body on the table. The cat had either recently been killed, or it had been dead long enough for rigor to release. There were no maggots, so my guess was newly dead. I admired Harvey's careful, almost reverent touch.

Death By Catgut

When life released its hold, a body relaxed. No more wrinkles, no more spasms of pain, no more cries or whimpers, no more muscle tension. Holding a dead animal in your arms wasn't like carrying a sleeping child. I learned at the vet clinic how to wrap a beloved pet in a towel to help with body support. It did not do the heart any good to have a companion go tumbling out of my grasp and onto the floor. Maneuvering a two-, or twenty-, or two-hundred pound flaccid bundle of flesh was a difficult skill to acquire.

When I entered his workshop, Harvey had some papers spread out on his table. He shuffled them together and put them under a book before I could read what they were. If I weren't hung over, I'd snoop.

Maybe later.

My housemate reached for his scalpel. Before he made an upside down Y incision in the cat's abdomen he petted her head and whispered, "Thank you."

"Can you cut quieter?" I asked.

He smirked.

"Why upside down Y?

"I'm focused on the stomach and intestines. This kitty had herself a birdy before she died." He hummed, "There's four little fingers, or is it four little toes? Only one birdy leg, no beak, and a good size hairball ready to disgorge."

"Way too much information, roomie." I held my hand over my mouth. Normally, I didn't mind what Harvey did with his spare time. We had a mutual respect of each other's space. However, doodling with catgut under the current circumstances weirded me out.

Harv stalled in his work and snickered, "A TMI alert from our town's Miss Share-It-All? Really?"

"Hey now, Judy is the psychic of note. I'm merely the hired help." I pressed my hand to my forehead, "Though I'm seeing a trip in your future . . . a visit to a small room. Wait . . . there's sunlight streaming in through . . . the bars!"

"Ha, ha. You're funny." Harvey said. "I'm doing this because of your cousin."

"You are trying to get us arrested, right?" I asked.

"No. I'm trying to find out if it's actually possible to strangle someone with real cat gut," he explained. "Or, if the coyote that got to Jimmy had a cat appetizer before his main course."

"Yew. More to the point, why would anyone do such a thing?" I wondered.

"Indeed." Harvey started cleaning a small stretch of intestine.

Death By Catgut

"And if the sheriff stops by for brunch?" I continued harassing him while he hung a rinsed section of gut on a line above my reach.

"Tell him I'm making sausage," he said.

"It's not going to look good for us if Ross finds dried guts hanging in our attic. Remember, we are suspects of sorts."

He snorted his derision. "It's not the attic, it's my taxidermy studio. This is an experiment. And, I stopped by Ross's office this morning before I came home. He's interested in what I learn."

"You could have said that to begin with. I need a beer to wash this awful taste out of my mouth," I stated.

"Have you tried soap?" he teased.

I stuck my tongue out at him. Harv pretended to swipe my mouth with his gruesome gloved hands. I ducked out of his reach.

Leaving my tongue hanging out I shouted, "Th-quick, I need-th Purell!"

Ignoring me, Harvey cut out the tiny heart and weighed it. It seemed in that moment a sad measure for an organ to which we attribute so much emotional and physical power.

"Okay, ghoul-boy, I'm out of here. You can bury your own dead cat when you're done."

"No worries. This little one is not the first I've laid to rest in our pet cemetery. You're in charge of saying the blessing afterwards. And don't worry about Ross; this little one's DNA wouldn't match with what they found in Jimmy's neck."

"If you say, my creepy friend, but this is Angel Falls. We lack sophistication at the CSI level. You could be in jail before the law figures out all this freaky laboratory stuff. Claire and I could be sitting beside you."

"Sure, sure. Would you Google 'catgut' for me on that fancy MacBook Pro of yours?" He wanted to get back to his work.

"What?"

"Research," he explained.

"And how do you know about my MacBook Pro?"

"Cedric, our cat burglar," Harv explained. "He batted it out from under your bed months ago."

"Figures."

"He also drug out a little music box. Lucky, I caught him before he knocked it down the stairs. It looked like laser etching in the wood on the top. Pretty. When did Doc give it to you?"

"He didn't," I answered flatly.

"Oh?" Harvey kept exploring the cat's splayed innards.

"Doc sent it to a friend of ours who lives in Florida a

month before he killed himself. He asked Gary to put it in the mail it to me in the event something happened."

"When did you receive it?" Harvey asked.

"A week, to the day, after we found Doc's body. Did you look inside?" I asked.

"No. Should I have?" Harvey countered.

I swallowed past the lump in my throat. "It came with a short note. Doc being as enigmatic as ever."

"Should I ask you what it said?"

"It was a quote from a song that we liked. 'If I should live forever and all my dreams come true, my memories of love will be of you'."

I slid into a shadow in the corner and stood lost in the deepest darkness I had ever known.

Harvey had been with me in Doc's condo when I walked across the blue tarp left on the bedroom floor by the first responders and felt something under it. Hysterical, I ripped back the plastic. Flesh, putrefied adipose tissue, dried blood and clumps of hair that even the coroner could not scoop out of the carpet lay underneath. I stood in the center of a perverted Jackson Pollock original and stared at the gore. I dropped to my knees frantically wading through my lover's scraps. Three weeks dead, the skin from his hands had sloughed-off and melted into the shaggy rug along with chunks of his scalp and sinewy tissue not held together by his clothing. I clawed through his ruins until I found his promise ring. One half of matching bands we wore to celebrate and our year-and-a-day vow. A ring he had taken off. Doc died with the titanium band back on the wedding finger of his left hand. I sat down in the middle of that floor design from hell covered in dried blood and body debris. I clung to the token of my broken dreams in my trembling hands, and cried until I couldn't feel anything. Anything at all.

Harvey took me home, and washed the horror off my catatonic body. The biohazard team came the next day. I didn't go back. In my anguish I slipped a small bit of hair, and a sliver of blood-soaked wood into my pocket. People did strange things in a state of shock. Those macabre tokens were hidden in a drawer inside the music box.

Doc made me a widow, but never a wife. Maybe everyone was right: time for this to be over. Jimmy, a dead cat, and me made three.

Death By Catgut

Catgut

Down in the kitchen I began preparation. Claire was coming for lunch. I had splurged with the extra money I made at last Friday night's card readings and bought steaks: one for Mutt, two for the kitties to share, and three for us adults. I finished my first beer and completed the salad by the time Harvey joined me in the kitchen. He was clean and shaven.

"Mister, you clean up nice. Are you wearing cologne?"

He stammered, "I didn't want to smell like dead catgut."

"Yeah, right. Go toss these steaks on the grill, and you can smell like dead cow. Claire will be here any minute."

Ooohhh.

After lunch, the middle-aged and joint-challenged humans, sprawled on the media room floor using pillows for furniture, while Mutt and five of his feline friends snoozed on the sofa. Claire brought the DVD of *Cats, the Musical* with her

157

for our entertainment pleasure. She and I sang all the songs in two-part disharmony -- loudly, proudly. Harvey and the sole representative of the canine species howled in complaint. We watched the show on my computer. Not exactly a theatre experience, but we went with what we had.

Guess it's time to break down and buy a flat screen.

"We're out of popcorn." Claire rolled over and groaned. "Someone help me up before the second movie. To be fair, I brought *All Dogs Go To Heaven*."

"I am ever the gentleman." Harvey stood, and extended his hand. "I'm done with popcorn. How about ice cream?"

I shook the almost empty popcorn bowl looking for old maids. "You're a wicked man."

"Yes." He smiled.

"Before I jump into a bucket of Rocky Road, or dare I hope, Double Dutch Chocolate Chip, tell me about the dead cat-in-a-bag," Claire said as she stretched the kinks out of her back.

Harvey gave me a dark stare.

I shrugged. "It's not like she doesn't know how we live here. We don't sacrifice small animals on nights with full moons. We don't have any human body parts buried in the basement."

"You don't have a basement," sniped Claire.

"Details!" I reminded her, "You're a suspect in Jimmy's murder, too. It's not only us at Hilltop under the microscopic eye of the law."

Harvey launched into an explanation of catgut before Claire and I could take our tangent any further. Harvey had an analytical mind to the N-th degree. He reached for one of his sketchbooks with anatomically correct animal drawings, their musculature and bone structure displayed in various stages of wholeness. I scrabbled to my feet. I reached for the book seconds too late and inches too short. Claire actually looked interested as he opened the tome, and began to show her his etchings.

"What we call catgut is not intestines from a cat," he said pointing to some drawing in the art portfolio. "It's a fibrous material found in the walls of animal intestines, usually sheep or cows. Ross told me the coroner found real cat gut in Jimmy's neck wound. I'm doing an experiment to see if I can dry an actual piece of cat intestine that is strong enough to be used as a garrote."

"Wait," I interrupted. "I'll get the treats while Mr. Science explains. Come on Mutt, potty break." I left them engrossed in morgue talk. Or was it engrossed in each other?

Mutt and his kitty entourage followed me toward the

stairs.

Claire whispered, "Tomorrow's the twenty-eighth."

Beyond Harvey's response of, "Yeah," I didn't wait to hear more. The hell with ice cream, I wanted a beer. We'd left the radio on downstairs. I walked into the kitchen in time to hear the words, "Wasted Days and Wasted Nights" blasting away. The radio sat on top of the fridge. To turn the song off I'd have to climb on a chair. Easier to leave. I bolted from the kitchen trying to out run myself.

A genius IQ, and all the counseling in the world couldn't save me from tomorrow.

#

Mutt, Mittens and I found ourselves sitting on Judy's back door stoop. Marmalade opted to stay at Hilltop. My beer was empty, and I wanted another. Mutt made a wolfie sound. I knew Judy stood behind us.

"You going to sit out there all afternoon, or you want to come in?" Judy asked through her screen door.

"Depends."

"Depends on what?"

"On whether or not you have more beer." I held my empty bottle up for her to see.

"Come on in."

160

Death By Catgut

We sat at her dining room table. Judy's house always smelled like fresh baked bread of some kind. Today, the aroma of cinnamon rolls wafted in the air. I helped myself to a bun and a beer. Judy sipped on sparkling water.

"So, what's on your mind?" she asked.

Sometimes a doctor needs a doctor. Sometimes a psychic needs a psychic.

"Same ol' -- same ol'," I managed to say. Jimmy's memory washed over me when I mimicked his response from our last meeting. Pecans and sticky rich icing smacked my lips together with each word. It wasn't a lie. I'd been at this mental place before.

"Any news on Jimmy's case?"

"Harvey's drying cat gut in the attic," I explained.

"One of your family?" I could see tension around her eyes.

"No, road-kill Harv brought in for an experiment."

"Death is difficult to deal with no matter how it reaches us."

"If you're going all sage-y on me, I need another beer and another cinnamon roll." I peeked under a cake cover on the table.

"Nan, outliving a loved one's natural death is like a

161

surviving heart attack. If you take care of yourself, the odds are good that you can pretty much return to a normal life afterwards. Suicides in your family are more like brain surgery." Judy took another sip from her sparkling water. "Even with great doctors and the best care, there's only a fifty-fifty chance that all your pieces and parts will function the way they did before."

I blew a heavy breath through my sticky, pursed lips. "Functioning parts are overrated." I wiped my hands on one of her cloth napkins and concentrated on peeling the label off my second longneck. If the paper came off in one piece, I got to make a wish.

"As you know too well, many suicides have a domino effect on those souls closest to the epicenter of death," Judy's tone turned soft and soothing.

I nodded my agreement.

"But betrayal, dear one, is like diabetes," she continued. "It's an incurable disease that takes away your ability to taste the sweetness in life."

I'm not sure what expression my face froze in when the truth struck me. My gut readied a purge in both directions.

"Excuse me," I rushed out of the kitchen.

Her bathroom design held to the philosophy of the more butterflies the better: wallpaper, hand towels, metal wall art and even small butterfly hand soaps. It smelled like baby powder, but not for long. Thankfully, Judy had air freshener and mouthwash conveniently placed on the counter.

Note to self: beer and cinnamon rolls great going down. Coming up, not so much. The beer sours and the cinnamon burns.

I looked almost presentable when I returned, except for the wet spot on my shirt where I rinsed out vomit.

"You need to eat," she suggested.

"I did." My voice sounded more defensive than I intended.

"Yeah, last week?"

"I had steak for lunch."

Judy made me scrambled eggs. Soft, easy on the stomach. Having left most of what I had eaten earlier in the commode, the eggs were welcome.

Judy moved the beer bottles to the counter and poured me a glass of sparkling water. "What do you want, Nan?" she asked. "What do you really want?"

I didn't answer. I concentrated on the scrambled mess in front of me.

"You're not afraid of dying. That much I know. Answer me this: why are you afraid of living?"

"I can eat or talk. Which do you want me to do?"

"You've always been good at multi-tasking."

I put my fork down. "I want my mind to stop screaming at me, and I want my heart to stop . . ."

"Beating?"

"Hurting," I corrected.

"Nice life if you can get it," Judy mused. "Dear one, most people have ghosts in their lives."

"Not like I do," I declared.

"True enough. You're aware of veil crossings more than most," she acknowledged. "You've gotten an advanced degree in sorrow. But, do you want to live the rest of your life only feeling sadness?"

"'No,' would be the easy answer here, but I'm holding out for 'numb' as a second choice, maybe 'I don't give a crap' as a close third."

"We've been here before."

I put my plate in her sink, and leaned against the counter with crossed arms. "Oh, yes. I've got the frequent flyer points from this destination, the tee shirt, the gimme cap, the free coffee mug." This game of truth or dare gripped my ass. "And, I'm certain I sent you postcards from each of the Seven Rings of Hell."

"Stamped in tears and post-marked with blood."

"Why are you badgering me?" I asked.

"Because I made a promise to you, that you probably don't even remember. I promised to be your voice of reason, when you couldn't speak for yourself. Do you like the view from this gloomy place you've put yourself in?"

I didn't answer her.

"Grow from the knowledge," she continued, "then let it go."

Anger flashed through me. "I cannot believe you! Did you really spout a platitude at me? Learn it. Live it. Let it go!" I stomped to the door. "I expect more from you."

"And I from you," Judy's gentle voice admonished me. "I remember what tomorrow is. Do you?"

"I'm so damn glad everyone is keeping up with the calendar for me."

"Time to make a choice, Nan. Be about the business of dying, or get on with the experience of living." It sounded somewhere in between a request and a challenge.

I gave her a wave, over my shoulder, minus four fingers. "Come on, Mutt. Where's your cat?"

"Nan," Judy yelled from her doorway, "while you're at it, try a different insulin." She clinked two empty beer bottles behind my back.

I did my version of an up-yours jig, and I danced my way out of her sight. *Where to now? I'm almost out of places to run from.* "Bar and Grill?" I asked Mutt.

He barked his delight and led the way. Mittens kept pace. It was doggie teatime. Mutt and my cat knew where Claire kept the treats. So did I. No surprises, the B & G was empty. Claire was having difficulty re-opening after JD's departure. Not from a business standpoint, she could get another cook, but from an emotional one.

Mutt gobbled down two imitation bacon strips while Mittens mobbed on a catnip infused goodie. I grabbed the open bottle of Crown, turned on the fake fire logs, and curled up on the faux stone hearth. Something beyond me felt odd. Dust motes floated in the muted beams of light streaming from the two skylights. The furniture was scarred, but with the neon beer signs off it passed for what designers called vintage distressed.

Mutt and Mittens cuddled together at my feet. I scratched Mutt's belly with my foot contemplating the fate of the world, the state of the union, and whether or not I wanted to see the sunrise tomorrow. Brooding took energy and depleted me emotionally, but I was damn good at it.

Everyone needs a hobby.

Death By Catgut

When I read the healthcare brochures, I found out many survivors of a suicide made deals with the Grim Reaper. I set the five-year anniversary of Doc's departure from his mortal coil as my date with death. I figured that would give me enough time to take care of all the estate legalities from him and Mom, put my own affairs in order, and finish whatever insignificant projects I needed to complete in my life. I promised myself I would do my best to search and rescue my soul without him, but if that was not possible, I allowed my broken spirit an opt-out point in time and space, a.k.a. tomorrow.

I hit the bypass stitch on the jukebox and punched in number ninety-three, by Garth Brooks, the extended version of, "The Dance." I waltzed alone with my ghost.

All my failures played in my mind. It didn't matter when in my life I'd made a mistake. The curse of imperfection sang my frailties over and over. I was totally disappointed with the way my life turned out. This breathing, heart beating, being up for the challenge charade had continued beyond reason or purpose. The whole point of the song lost on me. All of my dreams were gone. I didn't want a tearoom where people read poetry and ate pie. My great American novel got used in the cat boxes a long time ago. My balance had grown too bad for me to put on a pair of point shoes. The winter white dress and veil in the back of my closet would never be worn.

Disappointment became depression. Depression became despair. And, despair was only a dance away from death. Old Grimmy and I had a date tonight, at midnight.

I finished the bottle of Crown Royal, and passed out on the floor. Lucky for me, I woke up about forty-five minutes later in a puppy pile on the floor with Mutt and Mittens. Thank God we were curled up on the rug, not the barroom floor.

Been there, done that.

I left Mutt snoozing, but grabbed my big orange Maine Coon in my arms and staggered out. I arrived home to a dark house. My housemate and the regular kitty entourage were nowhere to be found. I tromped through the kitchen expecting to be accosted by whiskers. To my surprise, plaintive mews did not bombard me, except for Fidget. He came bounding into the kitchen demanding more kitty kibbles. An accomplished yodeler, his motto was "Be persistent. Be loud. And food will come." I couldn't fault his logic because it worked. I threw a handful of dry food in a bowl, and headed for the shower. I needed to clean the day off of me.

#

A couple of minutes after midnight, I climbed out onto our third floor roof and prepared my altar. I set the music box from Doc on a weather-beaten TV tray. Tears formed in the corners of my eyes as it began to play "Für Elise." I lit a white candle, the wick deep enough to stay burning in the breeze of the witching hour. I opened the box that held Doc's ashes. I drew a circle on my forehead with them. I had four of the five elements of life: music/air, candle/fire, ashes/earth, and tears/water. My life's blood after I jumped would represent spirit.

I poured myself some wine, and swirled the cabernet to the edges of my hammered copper goblet. Copper left a bitter taste in the wine. It seemed appropriate. I walked to the edge of our party balcony. Three stories were high enough to reach terminal velocity. Like a weather sock in a tornado, my waist-length calico hair blew about me. I opened my arms to fly.

"I'll be there in a minute, my love," I said out loud. "We've got things to talk about."

"Really?"

I startled. It wasn't Doc's voice that I heard from behind me. I glanced over my shoulder to see Harvey holding Punkin in one arm. She didn't like the wind and chitted at him like she did at naughty bluejays. I kept my back to them. I didn't know if I would have the courage to jump if I looked into their eyes. I was being selfish, like Doc, I knew it. The pain had won.

"In your 'Hello Kitty' pajamas? You're going to kill yourself in cat PJs? Like I don't have enough guy-grief to deal with living with you and fifteen cats. Go ahead. Jump. I'm getting a dog." Harvey sucked air between is teeth.

"Go back downstairs, Harvey." My voice rang hollow in my skull.

"Nan, if Doc were standing here, right now, and he said 'I'm sorry I hurt you,' would you forgive him?"

I didn't even have to think about it. "Yes."

From behind me Harvey's voice came out barely a whisper. His words swirled around me a gentle kindness, a virtual hug, a lifeline, if only I'd grab on. "If you would forgive him in life, then you have to be willing to forgive him in death."

"He's dead. Forgiveness doesn't matter to him, Harvey."

"It matters to you."

"Does it? Does anything matter anymore?"

"Before taking the big step, look at me. Damn it, Nan Elizabeth Ruth Atkins, you look at me," desperation crept into his voice. "How am I going to explain your death to your little orange companion? Punkin woke me from a perfectly splendid dream where I was . . . wait for it . . . da, da, da . . . Superman, I mean Super Grocer!"

We reflexively said together a line from *The Incredibles,*

"No capes."

Damn it, he made me laugh. *It's difficult to jump off a building when you're laughing.* I turned around, but didn't back away from the edge.

Harvey shook a box of Vermont Maple candies that he held in his other hand. He and Punkin were not playing fair. Harvey knew I could not resist a needy cat and sugar. He rattled the box again, and I walked toward them.

How can anyone commit suicide when there are maple candies in the world?

Punkin lurched at me. She trembled as I turned her upside down, and rubbed my tears off on her silky underbelly.

I whispered, "I'm sorry, heart-of-my-heart, to have put you through all of this." I raised my head to say I was sorry to Harvey, too. Then it happened. My heart let go. My knees weakened, and I fell with Punkin in my arms. I laughed. Harvey rushed to my side. He thought me hysterical.

"Nannie, I'm sorry. Oh God, I didn't mean to torment you. If you have to go be with Doc, I won't stop you. I promise, I won't make you stay. Nan? Nan!"

Sitting on our roof, in my Hello Kitty PJ's, with my crazy-lady hair blowing all around, and my comfort cat snuggled securely in my arms the life-threatening despair

171

dissipated.

Magick, redemption, grace, call it what you will. I took my first breath in years without a full mind- and body-ache.

I smiled up at Harvey. "I'm okay."

"Yeah, yeah, sure, sure."

"No, Harv, I'm really okay."

I leaned back against the pitch of the roof and gazed at the stars. A palpable pain in my chest still existed, but my sense of desolation, hopelessness was gone. Harvey joined me in lying against the slanted roof. Punkin rooted between us using our bodies as a wind block.

"You're okay-okay?" he asked.

I searched inward for any deep-seated, open misery and found only a memory scar. "Yes."

Harv's long arms reached over me and grabbed the bottle of wine. "How do you know?"

"This isn't only the anniversary of Doc's suicide," I explained to him and myself. "It's my expiration date." I let that sink in. "And I didn't jump."

I'd taken my first step toward living with the pain, rather than dying with it.

"Fine by me."

"I didn't hear you come home," I said.

"You were in the shower. You made all kinds of noise climbing up here with all this stuff." He gestured to my assembled altar. "I know what today is." He kissed the top of my head. "Nan, I miss Doc too, but I would miss you more."

"Thank you."

The music box wound down and the last notes played out.

"What now?" he asked.

Whew, that's the million-dollar question. Baby steps, Nannie.

"Now, give me the damn box of candy."

Catacombs

It might surprise my friends and family, but I have decided not to follow in Mother Teresa's footsteps. I'd nominate myself for sainthood, but I kept mixing my Hail Mary's with my Goddess Blesses.

Sue me, I'm like the early Christians. I accept crossover holidays.

Getting sober was easy. Finding reasons to stay sober, not so much. I actually liked the taste of Honey Nut Cheerios with Sam Adams Cherry Wheat. Lactose free milk made a poor substitute for flavor. After eating half of my bowl, I put it down for eager kitties.

When Harvey walked into the kitchen, it became apparent my curmudgeon housemate was having a "bad hair day." The edges of his cowlick stuck out on top of his head like devil horns. He stumbled into the kitchen half-asleep, stepped on Nutmeg's tail, and spilled his cup of hot coffee down the front of his shirt. He threw his mug in the sink, and let out a string of profanity that startled the other cats, and me.

His use of four letter words would have made my daddy proud.

The train wreck continued as Harv stubbed his toe on the counter, tried to compensate for too much forward momentum by flailing his arms, and fell backwards on his butt with a loud thump. There he remained. Nutmeg retreated to the safety of a corner, and licked his tail.

"Want some Beerios?" I asked pouring out another bowl.

"No, thank you," Harvey replied.

"Want to borrow my brush? You've got this sort-of swirly thing going on at the back of your head."

"No thanks."

"You want . . ." I started.

"NO!"

To a Peeping Tom, we would have looked like a sitcom kitchen diorama. The crazy lady at the dining room table shook a box of cereal, and seven cats played leapfrog for their spot at the bowl of milk on the floor. After his well-executed pratfall, Harvey sat. Harvey sat on the floor not moving. Harvey sat on the floor not moving, and not saying anything. I always lost waiting games.

"Soooo, did you poop your pants? You want I should leave and you can do the bathroom waddle without torment?" I asked.

"No, but . . ."

"What?"

"I think I broke my coccyx," he reluctantly admitted.

"I beg your pardon? You broke your what?"

"You know what a coccyx is. Damn it. I think I broke my tailbone."

I tried. I really tried not to laugh, but I failed. "You think you broke your ass?" I snorted. "OMG, alert the media – Harvey's butt is busted."

"Nan, if you don't shut up, I will hurt you. When I can move again," Harv threatened.

I noticed tears forming in the corner of his eyes. My own were from laughter, but I assumed his were from pain. I curtailed my teasing, and helped him up.

Between us Harv and I had half-a-car. I didn't mean we owned half a car, and the bank held the rest. Harvey had the title. I meant it literally, we had half a car: an old, convertible VW bug that didn't start off that way. The modification and welds that held old Betsy Mae together were inspiring if not artful. I didn't remember the original year model. BM had pieces and parts on her from several years, all in related, but not matching, shades of green. She was a wannabe dune buggy.

This year's inspection sticker was not only outdated, but probably impossible to pass. I sent a small prayer up to the traffic gods that no one with a badge, my cousin in particular, would pull us over on the way to the med clinic.

I put a pillow down on the wire seat for Harvey. He gingerly lowered himself in and down. Two hours, two x-rays, and two pain pills later, I had him, and his cracked coccyx, comfy in the media room, on the sofa with a doughnut pillow and four cats. I figured he'd snooze most of the afternoon. I headed for the Bar and Grill to tell tall tales.

#

At Claire's, I noticed a "For Sale" sign in the window, and a new guy in the kitchen. He appeared to be a middle-aged man with his greying hair pulled back in a ponytail. He wore a clean white apron, and bright yellow gloves.

"Who's that?" I asked scooting onto my favorite barstool.

"My new cook," answered Claire. "Glen meet Nan. Nan meet Glen."

Glen didn't come out to shake. He raised a gloved hand and did a grease covered beauty pageant wave, then went back to his task.

"He's cleaning!" I mouthed to my best friend.

She nodded and continued to mix a canister of fresh sweet tea. "You want a beer?

"Not now."

She arched her eyebrow at me, but said nothing. I poured myself a glass of sweet tea. It tasted good. It would have tasted better if it had been a Long Island Tea, but I needed to drive to the county courthouse this afternoon to dig in the real estate archives. My MacBook Pro didn't lack in skill, but what I wanted to find had not been computerized.

"You here to help organize Jimmy's memorial service?" Claire asked. "Ross said he was delivering the remains to the family."

"Cremains," I corrected. "Remains equals body, cremains equals ash."

"I figured we could hold the service here sometime next week. We can do it in between lunch and dinner. Maybe display Jimmy on the bar."

"What the hell?"

"Hey, you're the one who's had a dead man under your bed for years, so don't be pointing any fingers at me."

"Yew. It sounds bad when you say it that way."

"Um-hum. I'm just saying . . ."

"Why is Ross the one taking Jimmy to his family?" I asked. "Joe could have picked him up from the funeral home in Zoerne."

"I think Ross took the 'cremains' by because he had questions he wanted to ask Jimmy's cousin," Claire stated.

"You going to tell me about the "For Sale" sign in the window?"

"Reader's Digest version: It's time for a change," she admitted.

"And the long version?" I asked.

"Will take more than a glass of tea." Claire wiped off the bar top for the third time. "Glen is from the temp agency over in Zoerne. He's got some good ideas for an updated menu. My real estate broker said, it'd be better to have the place a working bar and grill again before I put it on the market."

I hate change. It gives me diarrhea.

"Want to do lunch tomorrow?" I asked. "We can over-share."

"That'll work," Claire answered.

"Would you look in on Harvey this afternoon?" I asked, "I've got an errand to run, and he broke his butt. Nutmeg helped him fall, and is feeling pretty sorry about his tail too."

"And you want me to what? Rub their tails?" she asked starting to snicker.

"Don't use Ben-Gay . . . on Nutmeg. Can I borrow your vehicle? I pushed my luck driving Harv to the doc-in-the-box in the BM mobile."

She tossed me her keys. "Oh, I almost forgot, your brother called here looking for you."

"Which one?"

"Zachary. He said he tried the house, but no one answered. Must have been while you were at the doctors. I told him you were fine."

"You didn't lie. I wonder why he called? Postcards are more his style."

"He didn't say. Probably checking on his baby sister."

"I hope nothing's wrong on his end." A twinge of guilt hit me. I hadn't asked the dragons about Zach's future in a long time.

"He sounded okay. Don't borrow trouble that isn't there. So, Harv's got a hurt hinny. What am I going to do with that man?"

"What you do with all of them." I pointed to her jar of past lovers on the counter. I left her trying not to choke on laughter.

Death By Catgut

#

The Appraisal District and Tax Office resided in the basement of the four-story, raspberry brick county courthouse over in Zoerne. I meandered through forgotten catacombs of cardboard. The dust bunnies were vying for dominance among the rows and rows of boxes and boxes. I liked the smell of old books, not the combination of old cardboard, silverfish dust or roach poop. I wanted a copy of the deed to Jimmy's gas station. I would have liked a copy of Jimmy's Last Will and Testament, but I wasn't sure he had one. His cousin Joe could have filed an unchallenged Quick Probate.

I'd been reading the *Angel Falls Chronicle* for a "Notification to Debtors" and found no legal posting. Maybe it was too soon. I didn't remember how long it took me to finalize Doc and Mom's paperwork. Those first three years after their deaths were a total mental blur. And the last two years I only had big event recall. All the little moments had slipped away.

No one had been in this part of the basement in a while. "Yew," did not describe my feelings as I brushed the cobweb from my calico locks. "Time to dye," I thought to myself when a few grey strands tangled on a cardboard corner. "And time to go."

Three hours in the box bowels, and I'd found the title

from when Jimmy's great-great-great-grandfather purchased the land after the Civil War, but not a lot of other information. The gas station wasn't built until the 1920's by another generation. I did not want to think about how many EPA regulations the old equipment might be in violation of. Since it stayed in the family, I expected safety exemptions had been "grandfathered" in, so to speak. I didn't find the transfer deeds from Gramps to Jimmy's dad or any paperwork thereafter. As far as the Appraisal District knew, Gramps Jackson remained the sole proprietor.

I did find out that Jimmy had an uncle who went "missing" shortly before his grandfather died, thus leaving all the family property to Jimmy's dad. Jimmy lost his grandpa, but his cousin Joe lost his grandpa, his dad, and his inheritance in short order. If I did the math right, Joe was around ten-years old at the time. That was awfully young to face his first round of "threes."

#

I felt a sense of accomplishment. My afternoon of research hadn't produced any answers, but it clarified some of my questions. I was ready to share my discoveries with Harvey and Claire. Laughter came from the second floor punctuated with an occasional, "Ow, eh-wu, ouch."

"I'm not sure I want to know what's going on up there!"

I shouted.

That sent the gigglers into another round. I found Harvey and Claire in clown face makeup. Toby watched them from the back of the sofa, bemused by their antics.

"Been sharing your meds?" I asked Harvey.

"No, no," assured Claire. "It's a joke. You know, turn that frown upside down. I guess we got carried away."

"You're going to scare your patrons," I admonished my buddy in a fit of unjustified jealousy.

"Chill out, Jumper," Harvey snorted. "The new guy is navigating the party barge this evening with Laura's help."

"My niece can run the place with her eyes closed," Claire said with pride.

"Claire volunteered to cook dinner for us," Harvey smiled.

"Not in my kitchen, she's not. We don't have a smoke alarm!"

I stomped downstairs. Toby followed. I heard whispering, but no more laughter.

Jumper? That is so uncalled for.

I started slamming cabinet doors. Fidget swatted at invisible bugs in the kitchen window until I took a wooden spoon out and beat the bottom of the cast iron bean pot. He and two other cats bolted for the back door. Claire walked into the danger zone with a towel in hand that had half her makeup smeared on it. Snowball followed her in, jumped onto the Formica table, and wrapped her fluffy white tail over her front paws to watch us.

"You look like a silent movie horror goddess," I spit out. "Scary, girlfriend. Really scary."

"I can finish washing my face, and I'll be normal. I can't say the same for you. Where's this attitude coming from?" she asked.

"Normal is overrated." I grumbled.

I threw the bean pot into the sink, which made Snowball and Claire jump. The white cat bolted, but Claire crossed her arms over her expansive chest and stood her ground. I reached inside the spice rack and pulled out a half empty bottle of Jim Beam. Claire grabbed for the bottle.

"No-no. No way. Not now!" she stated flatly.

We grappled for purchase on the bottle, and started pawing at one another. I pulled her hair. She smeared the makeup towel in my face. All in all, it looked like a bad version of the fight scene from *Turning Point,* except that our fight ended with her sitting on my back, me in an arm-lock, with a broken bottle of booze wafting up from the kitchen floor instead of us laughing.

"Enough!" Claire hollered and pulled tight enough on my arm to make me settle. "What the hell has gotten into you?"

"Nothing!" I huffed through a spill of hair. I struggled beneath her.

"I give you high marks for self-pity, and girlfriend you can wallow with the best morbid-obsessive person on record, but you don't do mean well. You're not very good at angry either. Stop it, Nan."

"Get off me," I demanded. "Get off me."

Claire pushed up, and re-clipped her bleached-blond hair. I crawled away and blew my wayward hair strands out of my face.

I pointed a finger at my best friend. "I don't want you to add Harvey as another notch on your bedpost, or a clump of ashes in your lost lovers pot."

"Are you and Harv . . ." she asked.

"No!"

"You asked me to come check on him. And I did."

Claire stepped over the broken bottle of whiskey, and pulled two longnecks out of the fridge. I rolled over, and propped against the cupboard. She slid down the wall and handed me a beer.

"You really need a couple of lessons on how to bitch slap someone. You suck at it," she scolded me.

I held the cold peace offering to my forehead. I did not need or want a headache. "You're pretty good at it," I saluted her.

"Practice." She was disinclined to expand her answer.

"You ready to tell me what's going on, or you want the bell to ring on round two?" Claire asked flatly.

I let out a sigh. "I don't know what to do."

"To do about what? I need a little more information, please."

She finished wiping the clown goop off her face. She looked younger, softer with her hair tussled, and no makeup.

"Everyone is moving on," I stammered. "The Bar and Grill is for sale. Harvey is going back to school. Doc died and I didn't. Claire, what do I do without the heartache? I wore it like a badge of honor. I suffered because it was better than feeling nothing. This is a whole new kind of empty for me."

"Harvey's doing what?" she seemed surprised.

"Out of everything I said, *school* is the one word you focused on? I saw the paperwork in his study." I pointed up with three fingers to indicate the third floor. "He tried to hide it when he worked on the dead cat stuff, but I saw it anyway. You know, he left school with a 4.0 grade point. A semester or two of catch up coursework, and he can reapply to med school or vet school more likely. He's good at putting broken parts back together."

Claire took a long pull on her beer, "Dead reckoning."

"Dead what?"

"Out at sea, dead reckoning is the process of estimating your current position based upon a previously determined position."

"If you start talking about me being adrift in an emotion sea, round two of this smack-down will most certainly begin."

She put up her hands in a gesture of surrender. "I'm not that poetical. But, think about it and it will make sense. You're trying to establish your 'new normal' based on where we all were before Doc's death anniversary. Or should I call it your opt-out date?"

My best friend had her moments, and I listened. Tux came in through the cat door, sniffed at the whiskey, and head-butted me for some of my beer. I poured him a swallow into my cupped hand.

Claire continued, "The disadvantage of dead reckoning is that since your new position is calculated solely from your previous positions, errors in the process are cumulative, and mistakes in your positional fix grow with time."

"Compounded life miscalculations, based on the premise that I am not good enough to be loved," I whispered into the top of Tux's tail. "Harvey's right. Nothing lasts forever."

He shuffled into the kitchen doorway. He shifted his weight trying to ease the pain in his backside. "That's not what I said,"

"Is too," I said.

"Then it's not what I meant!" He hobbled in, sniffed the air like Tux, and gingerly set himself down at the table. He'd washed his face and combed his hair. "What the hell are you two cooking? It smells like a distillery in here."

I climbed up the cupboard, and went for the broom. Claire stayed on the floor. When I looked at her, she shrugged.

"Not my mess," she explained to Harvey.

Dead reckoning explained a lot, but wouldn't clean up the broken glass or broken dreams. That was up to me.

Catnip Cuckoo

We ordered two pizzas with extra Canadian bacon "on the side." Giovanni knew why we ordered extra meat, and always drew a cat's head on the box for the kitties. His son, Bobby, delivered the pies. We knew food had arrived when Max and Cricket came barreling around the corner.

"We're out back, Bobby!" I hollered.

Harvey wasn't imbibing because of the pain medication, but he opened an estate bottled Cabernet Sauvignon for Claire and me as we settled on the veranda.

Yeah right, we popped the spout of our red box-o-wine, and sat on the part of the back patio that had not crumbled into the ground with age.

The porch overlooked what had once been a creek that fed back into the river. If you walked along the defunct "shoreline" you could find fish bones. The fish weren't caught

189

here, they were prepared here, and then in the fullness of time their unwanted parts had been blissfully washed away from the old cannery with the evening tide.

Not tide, more like big push from the paddlewheel.

The weather turned warm enough to sit outside and not be bothered by bugs. We weren't so lucky with cats. Whether they smelled the bacon or recognized Bobby's delivery car, we'll never know, but they showed up en masse. Seen all together we had quite an impressive pride.

Bobby took the roll of paper towels from the table and folded a few over his arm. Donning the demeanor of a maître' d, he pulled a Bic lighter from his pocket and lit our tabletop candle. He served the pizza with finesse to both human and feline connoisseurs. He finished by refilling our plastic glasses with vino, and took a small sip for himself.

We tip well.

"Say, Bobby, do you know Jimmy's cousin Joe and his girlfriend?" I asked.

"Not really," Bobby answered. "They don't order many pizzas. I've seen Joe at the gas station since . . ." Bobby paused, "since Jim died. Jerri Ann too, although she didn't look too happy to be confined to the cash register."

It sounded odd to hear him called Jim instead of Jimmy.

I guessed his contemporaries gave him a more grownup handle.

"I don't think they were close. Jim never mentioned his cousin when we bowled," Bobby added.

Claire wiped marinara sauce from her chin. "Jimmy bowled in a League?"

"Nothing formal. You know, a few of us kicking back on a Saturday night after the gas station closed and Pop shut down the pizza parlor. I think Joe only moved back to Angel Falls a couple of years ago. After his dad disappeared, he and his mom moved away. Joe's mom and his grandpa didn't get along."

"Really?" I wondered out loud. "I thought Joe was Jimmy's only family."

"As far as we know," Claire said.

"Doesn't mean they liked each other," Harvey chimed in as he tossed me a pizza bone.

I dunk the crusts in red wine.

"I heard you were going to have a memorial service for Jim." Bobby said.

I waved my hands to include everyone. "Planning committee."

We offered Bobby some pizza. The face he made had us all in giggles. I guess he had his fill of all things Italian with work.

"Let me know when you're going to do the thing for Jim. I'd like to be there."

Harvey paid him, and Bobby left promising the confederacy of cats there were enough goodies on the table for each of them to have seconds.

"What was that all about?" asked Claire.

"Not sure," I mumbled around my second pizza bone. "I don't want to sound like a headline."

"Murder in a small town is news," Harvey said.

"True. Death By Catgut is sin-sational!" Claire mispronounced the word on purpose. "Pour me more wine, please."

I looked to Harvey. "You got an update for us on the possible murder weapon?"

Rather than answer, he rocked in his seat trying to find a position that didn't put pressure on his broken backside. Nutmeg jumped into his lap to commiserate hurt tails. They did a yowling duet that ended with the big guy sharing his pizza with his singing partner.

"Where is your doughnut pillow?" Claire chided.

Harvey batted his big, brown eyes at her, and stuck out his lower lip. She jumped up to get it. I shook my head. They were headed for coupledom, no doubt about it. When Claire returned, and Harv had adjusted comfortably in his chair, he shared his catgut findings.

"From my little experiment upstairs I learned it's possible to strangle someone with cat intestines, if it's prepared correctly, but why? Why go to all the trouble of killing, cleaning, curing a piece of gut from any animal when a piece of string, a wire, a knife, a gun, or using your hands would be easier?

"Symbolic?" speculated Claire.

"For a catnip club, but for Jimmy?" I countered.

"Why does anyone kill?" Harvey asked.

"After the obvious reason . . . for food," Claire waved a piece of Canadian bacon at me. "There's always the seven deadly sins."

That set us on a round of guesses. We dismissed Vanity outright. Jimmy's life style did not scream high maintenance. He wore clean blue jeans, mostly flannel shirts, tennis shoes, and that awful baseball cap. He always appeared a month late on his haircuts and sometimes needed to be reminded to clean his fingernails. Jimmy was not narcissistic in mind, body, or deed. We ticked off Sloth and Gluttony quickly, paused a moment at Pride, and chuckled at Lust.

"That leaves us with Greed and Envy," stated Claire as

Sammie purloined a piece of Canadian bacon from her with stealth claws.

"Those two sins are a bad combination," added Harvey.

"Yeah, but it's Jimmy we're talking about here," I reminded them. "He would give anyone the shirt off his back if he thought they needed it. What would Jimmy be envious of?"

"Jimmy, is it?" a loud male voice blurted from behind me.

"Jesus!" I jumped straight out of my seat.

Claire laughed, "Another one saved, Lord, and we thank you."

I scowled at her and my cousin.

"Ross, you know better than to sneak up on people and cats."

I pointed three fingers at him, and told him to read between the lines. He hugged me anyway, and tipped his cowboy hat at Claire and Harvey. Ross shooed Tux out of the fourth chair at the patio table, and joined us. We offered him pizza and wine.

He raised the can of beer he in his hand. "Brought my own, thank you, but I will have some pizza."

"For shame, officer, drinking and driving!" I scolded.

"Not much."

"Not much shame or not much beer," I tormented him. "You're always welcome, but why are you here?" I asked putting two slices on a paper plate for him.

Ross didn't speak with his mouth full, but tried to use hand signals to answer.

Great, sheriff charades.

I pulled my ear and Claire joined in.

"Sounds like . . ." she said.

I hit my forearm with three fingers.

Harvey swallowed his pizza and added, "Three words."

I nodded. I strangled myself, waved and grabbed up Punkin to nuzzle in her belly fur.

Ross snorted, "Death by catgut. You are shameless, all of you. You are still part of my suspect pool. You know that, right?"

"Yeah, yeah. Your mouth moves and funny sounds come out," I teased. "Besides the fine dining, why are you here?"

"I picked up Jimmy and took him to his cousin, today. It was such a little box, a little plastic box. Not what I expected." He paused to finish his beer. When none of us spoke, Ross continued. "Something's not sitting right with me, and I want to run it past you."

"What is it, Cuz?" I snagged one of his pizza bones.

"Joe and Jerri Ann are not what I expected. The term trailer trash comes to mind." Ross spoke in hushed tones.

"You are getting dangerously close to profiling," I jokingly admonished him. "Was he wearing a 'wife beater' tee shirt and guzzling cheap beer?"

Claire added, "And was Jerri Ann wearing fuzzy pink house shoes with her hair in orange juice can curlers?"

"Does anyone still use curlers?" I asked.

"I'd focus on the fuzzy pink slippers," Claire continued.

"Pink, you say?" I wiggled my feet at her. "I could use some."

Harvey leaned over to Ross, "You're going to have to stop it. They can go on like this for hours. I've seen it happen."

My cousin shook his head. "Ladies . . . I noticed a collection of empty booze bottles scattered around the kitchen of their RV, but the thing that caught my eye was the shiny, diamond necklace around Jerri Ann's neck, and matching earrings."

"How many men know about matching earrings? I'm proud of you, Cuz."

Claire grasp her earlobe, "It's difficult to tell the difference between a real diamond and a good quality lab creation these days."

"Or the difference between a good riddance party and a wake," Harvey added.

"Yeah, I recognize that," Ross agreed. He washed his face with dry hands in a frustrated gesture. "Jerri Ann's smugness bothered me as much as Joe's rudeness."

"People grieve in their own ways," I interjected. "And, you tend to scare the hell out of most folks."

"I do not," Ross protested.

"You do too," I argued.

Claire, Harvey, and two cats nodded their heads up and down with me to confirm my cousin's daunting demeanor. Ross scooted away from the table with a grunt and kitties scattered.

"See what I mean?" I asked.

Ross stood up and did a full body stretch. He looked fine, but I recognized his body tension and decided to dial down the sarcasm.

"What's bothering you?" I asked. "Is there something specific?"

Ross walked into the kitchen without answering and came back with another beer.

Oh man, two beers. This is serious.

"When Joe tossed Jimmy's ashes on the top of the fridge, I saw his baseball cap behind an empty bottle of

Southern Comfort."

"Whose snap-cap you talking about?" Harvey asked.

"Jimmy came back to the bar to get his hat the night he went missing," Claire added.

"What's important about it?" I asked.

"Don't know," admitted my cousin, "but it wasn't with his body when we found him, and that's one of the things bugging me."

"Ross, it was an old gimme cap. I think you had one in high school. Does that make you a suspect too?" I asked.

"No," he stated emphatically. "Think about it with your witchy-weirdness, and let me know what thoughts come up."

I wiggled my fingers at him. "'Bibbity, bobbity,' boo-boo." I raised my eyes and hands in supplication to the sky, then down to him. "Nope, nothing . . . sorry."

Ross playfully smacked the back of my head. Our conversations went to Claire's new cook, and Harvey's new seat cushion, but we judiciously avoided talking about my new lease on life. Instead we debated whether or not it was too early or too late for Ross to spread Weed & Feed on the lawn. I warned him about the toxicity levels in relation to his dog. When the pizza disappeared so did the cats. The party broke up around midnight.

Death By Catgut

#

"What's going on?" I mumbled when Harvey and I met in the hallway at five-thirty in the morning stumbling toward the banging sound on our front door.

"We're coming!" shouted Harvey.

Harv took the stairs two at a time. I couldn't tell if he winced as he went. I looked like a Chihuahua running after a Great Dane. Harvey slept in boxers and bare skin. I guess he figured if anyone got him up at the break of day, they deserved the sight of his half-naked body.

Pretty damn nice for an old geezer.

I, on the other hand, wrestled with my Hello Kitty robe, and tried not to fall over Fidget, who assumed humans up equaled food given. Between robe ties and the orange kitten winding through my legs I got to the bottom of the stairs first.

"Shit, Nan, are you okay?" Harvey asked after making sure Fidget wasn't hurt.

"Yes, yes. Get the door," I pleaded.

The knocking continued and intensified. Harvey threw open the front door to find Claire standing on the stoop in a black teddy and a ratty old red sweater. She might have looked fetching save for the fact that she was bug-eyed, out of breath, and slightly damp from the early morning dew. Her feet were bare, muddy and bloody. She must have run all the way from her house to ours. Not sure what effect she was going for, but Claire had catnip cuckoo down pat.

For quick reference, catnip cuckoo comes after daffy-doodles and before bat-shit crazy.

Claire fell into Harvey's arms reaching for me to make a Claire sandwich. She trembled. We moved in tandem toward the kitchen. She didn't let go of either of us until we scraped her off and sat her at the table. I grabbed for a bottle of brandy. Harvey's backside showed no signs of residual pain as he ran upstairs for a blanket. Tear tracks traced down my best friend's cheeks. She looked up at me before Harv came back. Her eyes begged me for something I couldn't discern.

"You've got to give me a clue," I whispered, not letting go of her hand. "What's going on? What do you need?"

She gulped in the air around her like a drowning victim brought to shore.

"Nan?"

"I'm right here, sweetie," I soothed.

"Oh God, Nan," Claire shuddered.

Harvey returned with his bedspread, and draped it over Claire's shoulders. He'd found his jeans, but not a shirt. Under other circumstances, I'd have said he was showing off. I poured

Claire a shot of brandy in a dirty coffee cup that had been left on the table sometime yesterday. She gulped it down and rocked. I poured myself a healthy quarter-cup and downed it.

Harvey started checking her for wounds. "Are you hurt?" he asked, but it came out a bit harsh.

"Take a deep breath," I encouraged all of us. "Why did you knock?"

Our door was never locked. Claire was family. She walked in when she wanted, got what she wanted from the cupboard or fridge without asking permission. She had a toothbrush in my bathroom. Why had she been standing on our front porch banging on our door? Harvey sat on the other side of her keeping a calming hand on her shoulder. Punkin jumped on the table startling Claire. My little empathy cat purred loudly, and leaned into Claire absorbing some of her stress. I fretted silently that I was using up Punkin's soul energy with my own neediness. It had been a difficult couple of days, weeks, hell a difficult few of years for us all.

"Honey, what happened?" I asked Claire.

She leaned into Harvey for comfort, and squeezed my hand to the point of numbness.

"It's JD," she whispered.

"JD?" repeated Harvey, his voice hinting at territoriality.

I took Claire's face in my other hand, and focused her eyes on me. My heart ached as she nuzzled into my palm for comfort.

"What's going on?" I asked softly.

"JD's . . . dead," she choked out.

That makes three. I thought it would be Jimmy, the road-kill cat Harvey brought in, and me. It was JD instead.

"JD's dead," I repeated to see if she would correct me.

Harvey glanced at her nightie and pushed away from the table. He got up to dole out dry food and a dollop of Greek yogurt for the fur babies to eat.

"Claire, how do you know JD is dead?" I asked.

She hung her head. "I found him. Like you found Doc."

"You found him? You mean you found his body?"

"Where?" demanded my housemate.

"In my bedroom," Claire admitted.

The color drained from Harvey.

"In the closet," she explained.

When she said that the tension in Harvey's shoulders relaxed. A snicker escaped me. I tried to cover it with a cough.

"Last night when you got home?" I gaged.

"No, this morning when I got up to pee. I reached for my sweater," she tugged at her red wrap beneath Harvey's bedspread in case I hadn't noticed it upon her arrival.

Not sure why that image of JD on the floor in her closet was humorous to me, but it was. I pressed my hands over my mouth. *Inappropriate laughing and crying, thy name is Nan.*

"And there he was on the floor in my closet," she repeated.

"In the closet?" I snorted through my fingers.

"Will you stop saying everything I say?" Claire's eyes weren't buggy any more, but her voice shook.

In a surge of panic I asked, "Where's Laura?"

"At her boyfriend's."

"Are you sure?"

Claire only nodded.

"Where's Mutt?" Harvey added. "He didn't bark?"

She was unresponsive. She put her head on our table and sobbed.

If Mutt hadn't barked, or alerted her to an intruder during the night, that probably meant JD was in the closet when Claire got home. Mutt wouldn't have seen a dead JD as a threat.

Crap, crap, crap on toast with marmalade.

The room went silent. We weren't ignoring Claire's distress. We were processing it. That kind of announcement took a moment or two to digest. Harvey went upstairs to finish dressing, and dropped clothes over the bannister for Claire and me to change into.

When he came back into the kitchen he asked, "Did you call the sheriff?"

"No. I came straight here," Claire mumbled.

"Call him, now!" he barked.

"I'm going to wash Claire's feet, get her dressed, and put a little food in her. You call Ross, and explain to him what we think we know. Tell him Claire's a bit spacy on the details, and that we'll meet him at her house in a few minutes."

I was surprised how calm I sounded. I made toast. I wasn't going for gourmet of the year, just something besides bile and bourbon in our bellies. Harvey brought in the *Angel Falls Chronicle.* Headlines read that gas prices were going up. No mention of a dead ex-fry cook at Claire's house.

Fifteen minutes later, we stood in Claire's front yard waiting for Sheriff Ross and Deputy Ron to arrive. Noise from the squad car siren woke Mutt. He bellowed from the garage long after Ross turned it off. The commotion caused neighbors to wake, rise, turn on their kitchen lights, and gather on the porches that faced Claire's house. Without being told Ron began to string yellow crime scene tape around Claire's pecan trees marking off her whole yard. Ross headed inside with Claire and

Harvey. When I started to go with them, Ross motioned me back.

"I don't need anyone else corrupting the evidence," Ross said.

"Oh, please. My finger prints and hair follicles are all over Claire's place," I protested.

"On the body?" Ross asked pushing his hat up on his forehead so he could give me a hard-ass stare.

"You're letting Harvey go in." I felt a pout coming on.

"JD's a big man. I may need Harvey's help in handling the body."

Ross tossed a pair of rubber gloves at my housemate. Claire sagged at her knees, but she didn't faint. I'm not sure if the guys even noticed. I gave up arguing and sat on the steps to wait. Claire had a walk-in closet, but it would get crowded in there with fifty pairs of Payless shoes, a dead body, and the law.

Snookie, who lived next door to Claire, brought a carafe of herbal tea to the edge of the yellow plastic ribbon, and set it down in the grass along with a tray of mugs and muffins. She caught my eye and pointed to a small flask inside the cup with sunflowers painted on it. I think the glass vial was supposed to hold water for a single flower. I assumed it held a shot of vodka for me.

Bless you, Snookie Adams.

Deputy Ron and her talked over the yellow taped perimeter as I rose to retrieve the dish of goodies. I didn't have any information to add, so I didn't stay. I overheard the words, "not a coincidence" and "murder." I blew Snookie a silent thank you kiss, not wanting to interrupt their discussion. I wished I'd brought my cards to fidget with. I stared to weed the flowerbed and got a lecture from Ron to stop.

"Can I take Mutt for a walk?"

"No, ma'am. Not until we check him for evidence."

"Okay." I said, and went back to my perch on the porch.

Waiting sucks. I mean, how long does it take to find a dead man in a closet?

Why Doesn't Matter

I sucked poppy seeds out of my front teeth as Cody arrived to take photos.

Crap, crap, crap.

Cody's attendance meant JD was really in there, and really dead. I kind of hoped this unfortunate Kodak moment was a mistake. You know, maybe a dirty bundle of laundry that Claire forgot, and tripped over in in the dark of dawn.

"Morning, Miss Nan."

Cody's hair hadn't been combed. The sun rose above the horizon, but it was early by most people's standards. Ross had called him out of bed, no doubt. I'd been sitting here a goodly amount of time.

"Morning, Cody. Here are some lemon-poppy seed muffins from Snookie. They're good. I've had two, and it smells like Claire's made coffee in the kitchen."

"Much obliged." Cody broke a muffin in half, and swallowed it quickly. "Glad it only smells like coffee inside," Cody murmured as he walked passed me.

"Me too."

We had both seen more than our fair share of death. Cody in war; me in peace. His scars were more visible than mine, but then so was his healing. He wore shorts this morning and had his blade style running leg on. He didn't do marathons anymore, but he did fun runs for charity and two miles every day to keep the rest of him in shape. Failure was simply not an option for him. I admired that.

Harvey and Claire came out and sat beside me on the steps. Harvey had tears stuck in the corner of his eyes. Claire's tears were in a full slide down her cheeks.

"We're not supposed to go anywhere," Harvey told me.

"Are we allowed to check in with our employers?" I asked. "I actually have work at the vet clinic today."

"I am my employer," Claire sniffed. "All present, but not accounted for."

"I guess this moves us all up on the current homicide suspect list," I speculated.

"At least me," Claire acknowledged. "I could be the gangster maw and you two my posse."

Death By Catgut

Harvey teased, "More like the madam and her . . ."

"Hey now," cautioned Claire.

"The question's got to be asked. Why are you keeping a dead, ex-boyfriend in your clothes closet?" I tried not to snicker. "Wouldn't the big freezer at the B & G be better?"

Gallows humor.

"I'm not keeping him," Claire answered.

"I beg to differ," I countered.

"I've already heard this part. I'm going to get coffee. I don't want that herbal shit from Snookie. No offense meant," said Harvey. "I need caffeine in a bad way."

"A point of clarification, Harv, there is no bad way for caffeine: coffee, chocolate, diet cokes, intravenous. I accept all forms with gratitude and glee."

"Does that mean you want a cup."

"Please. The muffins are great though."

He went back inside. I put my arm around Claire. She shivered, but I didn't think she was going into shock. I asked her what her name was, where she lived, who she had in her closet, etc. She punched me, and I figured she was fine.

"What are they doing in there," I asked her.

"I left when they started to duct tape paper bags over JD's hands."

"They do that on TV to preserve any evidence that might be under his fingernails. You don't have any recent scratches? Do you?"

"No. What part of I found him dead in the closet this morning, do you not understand?"

"I'm making sure you keep your story straight. You're more lucid now than when you showed up at our house."

"Sorry about that."

"Don't be, that's what friends are for. But this finding dead boyfriends thing between us has got to stop. One a piece is enough."

"Agreed."

"You want to talk about it?"

"I think I told you everything. I stepped in my closet for this old sweater. I keep it on a hook inside the door. I stumbled over JD's big old boots. Nan, I swear to God if you say anything about him dying with his boots on I will really hit you."

I put my hands up in surrender. *There's gallows humor, and then there's bad taste.* "You didn't hear anything go bump during the night?" I asked her.

"No."

"Anything missing?"

"I don't think so," Claire looked over her shoulder. "I

didn't take time out to look around or check anything. I got the hell out. The events were pretty simple: get up to pee, stumble over a dead body, run to your house."

"Ross will probably ask you about your jewelry," I mumbled.

I hated saying that out loud. I didn't want to accuse Claire's ex-lover of being a petty thief, but I grasped for an explanation as to why JD lay sprawled amongst Claire's shoes.

"Do they think JD died in your closet?"

Claire shrugged. "According to Ross, there's not any sign of a struggle."

"In your closet how can you tell?"

She rabbit punched me. Okay, I deserved that.

"He's lying in there, passed out on my only pair of Prada pumps. They're old, but they're Prada. I swear, I'm going to be so mad at that man if he's ruined my shoes."

I hugged her. Fancy shoes were the least of her concerns, but I figured I should keep her talking.

"We don't know if JD was killed. Maybe he left something in your closet, and came back to get it, and had a heart attack or stroke before he could leave." I grasped at non-existent possibilities. We both knew it.

"Nan, with all your psychic abilities, why didn't you see

this?" Claire asked without accusation in her voice.

"I wasn't looking, honey. I'm sorry," I admitted, ashamed for my lack of foresight. "I was wrapped up in my memories of Doc, focused on my own destruction, I stopped shuffling my cards."

"Don't hang your head like a hand-beat dog. I mean beaten cat. I'm not blaming you. I sure as hell didn't see this turn of events either. Even if I'd had a heads-up from the realms beyond, I'm not sure what I could have done different?"

"Maybe not be here," I suggested.

"Better me to find him than Laura. It could have been her coming in to feed Mutt, or borrow a blouse. I wouldn't wish that on her."

I nodded my head in agreement. "Ross say anything to you?"

"Yeah," she laughed, "Go outside, sit down, and don't leave town."

"He's getting cranky."

I thought to myself, Ross was a piss ant to make this sound official. Then again, this was official. Claire leaned in, and put her head on my shoulder. She stifled a shudder. I kissed her on the top of her head, and wrapped her in my arms.

"Harvey is taking this all in a fairly calm manner," I

observed.

"He's been living with you the past five years. He's used to weirdness."

I tugged at her bed-head hair.

"Ouch, brat. Harvey realizes JD didn't come here at my request," Claire stated.

"I wonder why he came to your house?"

"Why doesn't matter," Claire said. "It doesn't matter in most situations. Something is or isn't. Knowing why doesn't bring any comfort, or change a damn thing."

"That's pretty heady for this early in the morning."

"I've been awake a long time."

Claire got up to stretch. She waved at the neighbors, and then held up the half muffin Cody left. "Thank you, Snookie. We'll tell you all about it when we can." Claire hollered to the neighbors in general.

The hearse and coroner arrived from Zoerne. We watched in silence as he and his assistant rolled the gurney inside.

"I didn't want JD to go when he did," she admitted, "but after he took his leave, I let out a breath I didn't know I'd been holding. I felt lighter, almost happy. JD was a negative sort of person. He had more than one chip on his shoulder." She wiped her nose on her sleeve. "I didn't want to say any thing to you, because you had other 'things' to deal with. He'd started acting secretive and moody, and except for taking Mutt on his walks, he didn't do much around the house. Don't get me wrong. He was a decent cook and decent in bed, but he was not my true love-life partner-soul mate. JD was just a warm way to pass last winter."

I cleared my throat.

"And, before you ask, I didn't leave our relationship with a 'stop by any time' invitation. Gone is gone, and done is done. I don't have a clue why he came back. You getting any," she made a swirly motion around my head, "messages from the great beyond?"

"We are experiencing a temporary difficulty with communications through the veil. All lines are down." I shrugged. "Sorry."

"Yeah. Aren't we all?"

"Claire, was JD strangled?" I asked.

My question surprised her. She didn't have time to respond before Ross, Cody, Harvey and the recently arrived coroner's assistant appeared in her doorway with a big black bag strapped to the gurney.

"We're going to move the body, Miss McCarthy," Ross

said. "Cody is done with photos. Ron and I will be a while longer, processing the crime scene and talking with the coroner. He's out in the garage with your dog, at the moment. When he's done you'll be able to feed Mutt and walk him. You can come into the kitchen if you like. We're going to have more questions for you, for all of you," he said looking in my direction, "before we are done."

"Crime scene?" squeaked Claire.

Those two words rules out JD having a shoe fetish with a happy ending in the closet.

As the gurney rolled by, Claire reached out to touch it, but Deputy Ron gently dissuaded her effort. She wrapped her sweater closer around her. Harvey stood behind us, and draped his arms protectively around us both.

Once the body had gone, the neighbors lost interest and went inside their homes. We followed suit, huddled in Claire's kitchen sucking down strong coffee while Ross and Ron finished fingerprinting and riffling through the house. I plundered the cabinets to add Bailey's Irish Cream to my cup. It felt like the beginning of a long, long day.

And it was.

At noon, Ross dismissed Harvey and me, pushing us toward the door. He and the deputy began to walk Claire through the house again. I heard him ask her not if anything was missing, but if anything had been added.

Added?

Harv and I took Mutt home with us so he wouldn't mess up any pertinent evidence. The Maine Coon brothers bounded in, happy to see their buddy.

"Look, one of my familiars brought me spell components."

Harvey huffed, "Not sure what you're supposed to do with two disembodied bird feet placed at our back door."

"They're a gift. And as an added boon, there's no blood or other regurgitated parts on the rug."

"Sure, sure."

He went upstairs to change. No cats remained to thank when I picked up the pieces, but I said it anyway. In my line of work and with Harvey's hobby, I couldn't afford to be squeamish around wounded or dead critters in parts or whole. Max brought in a baby raccoon last spring, but I fostered it out before Harvey took a notion to stuff it, and add it to our collection.

Kidding. We already have four stuffed raccoons. Who needs five, right?

"Why did Ross ask Claire if there was anything added?"

I wondered aloud while Harv made himself a sandwich to take to work with him.

"Maybe he was trying to see if JD, or our mysterious Angel Falls serial killer, set her up by leaving incriminating evidence behind. Or Ross could have been checking for inconsistencies in Claire's story. Sometimes lawmen ask the same question different ways to see if the answer changes."

"Serial killer?"

"Two dead in two months." Harvey stated.

"Claire didn't do it!" I almost shouted at him.

"Not what I'm suggesting, in any way."

I was stressed to the point of not knowing what to do next. Harvey came over, kissed me on my forehead and hugged me. I missed hugs from Doc. Safe in his arms I felt I could get through anything. A Harvey hug was the next best thing.

Harvey let go of me to finish packing his lunch. "Maybe you two middle-aged, *Avengers* wannabes could have taken Jimmy down, together. No offence meant, but you and Claire wouldn't have stood much of a chance against an ex-military guy, like JD. He was in good shape."

"Aren't you going to add 'for his age'?"

"For any age. The guy had guns and upper boy strength you wouldn't believe."

"We could have snuck up on him," I mumbled.

"Do us all a favor, and don't say that to Ross, cause from what little I saw in the closet, that's exactly what it looked like someone did."

"Someone attacked him from behind? Was he strangled?"

"Can't say. I don't think this is another death by catgut, if that is what you're asking."

"So what are we going to call this one? Death by Vera Wang?"

Harvey snickered.

"Say, you want to get on the good side of Claire? Buy her a new pair of shoes. Even if she thinks she can now, she's never going to be able to wear those pumps again. They will be way too heavy to walk in."

Harvey left for work. I had another cup of black coffee, and watched Mutt play chase-the-dog's-tail with several of the kitties. Two deaths in two months, it was a puzzle. Maybe I needed to ask the same questions a different way, but none of my senses, regular or otherwise, helped.

I called Claire's niece and left a message on her cell, telling Laura that she and Claire would stay at Hilltop for the foreseeable future. No arguments allowed. I knew she'd talk to

Claire before she got my message. I checked my watch. I had about forty-five minutes to Google Jimmy's family tree before I needed to be at the clinic. I wanted to add in a background search on JD.

Silly thing, I didn't remember his last name. My first stop would be the Bar and Grill to snag one of JD's old pay stubs. That would have his full name and his social security number on it. The B & G got a strong WiFi signal, one of the few in town. Fiber optics were coming, just not here yet. Snookie's muffins had worn off. I felt hungry. I could use Claire's computer. She always had Cheerios and beer on hand.

#

What I found with my limited Internet search did not make my Beerios settle easy. JD, a.k.a. John David Monroe, on the payroll stub, did not exist. Well, not with his reported birthday or social. As a matter of fact his social appeared to belong to a dead ten-year old girl named Jenna Denyse Monroe. It was simpler than I thought it would be to track down personal information. I subscribed to a couple of websites that let me plunge deeper into privacy grey areas. As long as I cancelled my accounts with the information sleuths within thirty days, my bank account wouldn't go belly-up in protest. The kitties need not fear for kibbles.

Naomi Patterson

If Miss Marple had had the electronics available today, her made-for-TV movies would have become thirty-minute after-school specials. A couple of mouse clicks, and I sped on my way to a personal invasion! Truth told, anyone could find out anything with a quantum of computer savvy and tenacity. Hackers Rule. (Or will someday.) My Granny Winnie's childhood warning came back to haunt me: "Be careful what you wish for." I wished for answers, but I did not like what I found.

I wanted to drink more, but the clinic had a neutering scheduled in an hour, and I had a grooming session after that. It was one of my rules to be sober for any activity that involved sharp objects. Poodles with punk hairdos were only funny when Johnny Depp was their groomer.

Why is this happening?

I didn't understand what to do with the information I gathered, hard copy or by witch-o-gram. When I read the Tarot cards for Harvey and Claire, what seemed like a lifetime ago, I turned over The Lovers card – duh. The Wheel of Fortune card fell upside-down which meant change – double duh. Their final outcome card was The Tower. That card denoted a circumstance beyond one's control wherein the questioner had no choice. I supposed a dead body in the closet qualified as a circumstance beyond one's control. As long as "said dead body" was put in the closet by someone other than the questioner.

I'm a lousy psychic. I see a tall, dark, stranger . . . in your future . . . in your closet . . . dead. Only I didn't see, anything.

I pulled my dragon Tarot cards out of my purse, shuffled them and laid out an untraditional three-card spread. It was designed to be down and dirty: past-present-future. The first card I turned over was The Death Dragon.

"No shit, Sherlock," I said to the empty bar.

I'd share a cup of tea or a shot of whiskey with either of the current big screen or little screen incarnations of the genius gumshoe: Robert Downey, Jr. or Benedict Cumberbatch. Their characterizations of Sherlock Holmes reminded me of Doc: beautiful, brilliant, arrogant, high functioning sociopaths, inviting and frustrating in the same instant.

So, not where I want to go with that thought this afternoon.

I grabbed up the cards and shoved them back in their weathered, cardboard container. If the Powers That Be wanted to speak to me, today, they'd have to find another way. The petty gods of circumstance weren't being rude; they were being mean. I had other places to be and, mercifully, other things to

221

focus on.

The rest of the day remained uneventful. The surgery was successful, for us. Yeager Meister, a Golden Retriever, would sleep the evening away and wake to a new life of less amorous activities. Murphy, a Shih Tzu, pranced home with her spring buzz cut and pink bandana. We had one drop-in for a puncture wound on a cat. She hadn't presented with an abscess yet, which made the wound difficult to find. I had to shave most of Itty-Bitty's backside. Eventually, we found a small hole. I held her as the doctor cleaned the wound.

"You've been running away from fights, little one," soothed Dr. Word. "Good for you. Run faster."

Why were both Jimmy and JD attacked from behind? Were they running away from a fight? Claire was right, why didn't matter, but maybe who or what did. I needed to go nose around the courthouse again.

Sometimes when you don't know what you're looking for, it's easier to find.

Death By Catgut

Knock-Knock

The Zoerne coroner determined JD had been killed around ten o'clock the night before he was found. Harvey, Claire and I breathed a sigh of relief. We had the best alibi on the planet. We were eating pizza and drinking beer with my cousin, the sheriff. We also learned that by all indications, JD's body had been moved into Claire's house after he had been bludgeoned. He did die from blunt force trauma to the back of his head.

Ross said his information had to do with body lividity, rigor, and the small amount of blood found at the scene. Ross could not, however, explain how JD's six-foot, one hundred and ninety-pound muscled body got moved into Claire's house without leaving drag marks of any kind. And they didn't have a clue what the murder weapon was, yet. Something metal and heavy.

"Did someone vacuum the carpet after pulling the body across the floor?" I asked. "That's a bit creepy."

"From you, that's saying something," Ross teased.

I gave him my best don't-piss-me-off glare.

"It had to be more than one person," Ross told me over morning coffee. "Moving that much dead weight is not for the weak or faint of heart."

"I can imagine," I whispered.

Ross patted my hand. As part of his rescue activities he'd carried bodies, alive and dead. Sadly, he knew what he was talking about. My experiences revolved around smaller beasties, except for one horse. That disposal involved a bulldozer. Of course, my mind immediately jumped to JD in a dozer scoop. I shook my head to make the image go away.

"Change the channel," I whispered to myself.

"You okay?" My cousin asked through pursed lips.

"Yup. A lot of miscellaneous noise in my brain these days." I assured him, "No pictures that would help you. So, you're scouring the countryside for muscle-bound, tag-team killers who travel with a Hoover?"

Yeah, I'm a smart-ass.

"I didn't say they cleaned up after dumping the body. The carpet didn't look vacuumed. I said, we didn't find any drag marks or shoe prints that didn't match in size to Claire and JD's. It's perplexing."

"Perplexing, good word. I like it. It's perplexing to me, why you asked Claire if she found anything. A dead JD doing a face plant into her flip-flop collection wasn't enough?"

"I'm not sure what we're looking for, Nan, and even if I knew, I shouldn't tell you. You're off the hook for JD's death, but Jimmy's case is cold, not old. Both of these are on-going investigations."

I punched him in the shoulder.

"Okay, okay. I don't think you killed anyone," Ross said. "But, that's off the record."

I picked a frying pan from the stove and threatened him. "The day is young."

He flashed me a charming smile, and I lowered my weapon. I bet that smile got him out of hot water with his wife on more than one occasion. He let out a long sigh or maybe it was a low growl.

"There's not a lot of material evidence to go on in either murder. Jimmy was three days dead in the woods, and he'd been chewed on."

A wave of nausea had my coffee yearning to be free. I hadn't thought about the being chewed on part. "So, the catgut was leftover from a coyote?" I asked in a whisper. "I thought when you said that, it was a morbid joke."

Ross shrugged, his frustration evident. "Investigations like these don't get resolved as easy as on TV. Most crimes don't get solved at all."

"I don't like the sound of that," I told him.

"You don't have to. I'm not partial to that outcome either, just aware of it as a possibility." He corrected himself, "As a probability."

Ross looked tired. He'd kept the peace in and around our town for years: found lost children, run-away dogs, helped rescue cats in trees, campers in jeopardy, broken up a few brawls and jailed a few drunks (not me). He dealt with death, but murders were out of his purview. We averaged a drowning per year, usually someone doing something stupid like jumping jet skis. Ross was a leader in the search and rescue/recovery teams in the county. He certified as a Dive Master in SCUBA, and qualified in advanced CPR every two years, but these two murder cases were more personal. He put pressure on himself that nobody else would. These were the first non-accidental deaths in Angel Falls in over three decades.

"You know, none of this mess is your fault or your failure," I told him.

Death By Catgut

"Back at you, Cuz." Ross blew on his coffee. "Sometimes when there's a knock on the door and you open it, all you find is an empty doorframe."

"Does that mean no one's there, or that we can't see them?"

Ross didn't answer me. He took a final swallow, and put his cup in the sink. His mama raised him right. As he left, he tried to lock the front door.

"Nan Elizabeth Ruth Atkins!" he bellowed.

Growing up in a southern family I could gage how much trouble I was in by what I was called: "Nan or Nannie" they were trying to get my attention or be endearing. "Nan Elizabeth" meant I had crossed a minor infraction of the rules. An apology and a promise of better behavior usually let me skirt any kind of corporal punishment. However, if I heard "Nan Elizabeth Ruth Atkins" I might as well bend over and kiss the stinky parts. "I'm sorry" didn't matter. I was going to pay for my conduct, or lack thereof, and dearly.

"On it!" I hollered back. *Locks-smocks.* "Yada, yada, yada."

"I heard that. If not for you, do it for me." His words wafted down the hall toward me. "Do it for the rest of your family. You don't want any of your cats to be hurt!"

How does he do that? Arrows straight to my heart.

I stomped down the hallway and rattled the deadbolt after him, making as much noise as I could. Guessed I shouldn't tell him most of the windows didn't lock, or that the quasi-basement door didn't even shut. Quasi, because it wasn't a real basement only an area under the stilts big enough to hold a freezer, a washer and dryer and a few miscellaneous boxes, but it had stairs that led to the main floor, and the door there was never locked either.

"That the sheriff?" asked Claire as she came downstairs in search of coffee.

"Yup."

"I smell nectar of the gods."

"The coffee is almost fresh, and waiting for you in the kitchen," I instructed. "Ground this morning. A dark, aromatic, French roast with real cream. Well, if the kitties haven't knocked the lid off the pitcher."

"Love ya." She tossed finger kisses back at me over her shoulder.

I wandered into what would someday be our downstairs living room or library or art gallery. At present we used it as a furniture storage area. Harv and I had delusions of grandeur when I bought the house. Expectations had been lowered in my life by grief. I settled for functioning indoor plumbing.

Pain did funny things to people, whether it was physical or emotional. When disappointments developed, dreams diminished. I blew dust from a box that read "Doc – bedroom" marked in Sharpie across the side. I had drawn an "unhappy" face with tears running down his face. In the corner I'd piled what I kept from Mom, and a rocking chair from Harvey's sister. I could have gotten lost in the maze of cobweb-covered cardboard containers, but Claire saved me from death by dust bunny when the sound of her house shoes scuffed up behind me.

"Love what you've done to the place," she teased. "It takes Shabby Chic to a whole new level. What do you call this?"

"Early American Disaster," I said.

"Modern Misadventure? No, no it's Distressed Eclectic Expressionism."

"How about French Provincial Blight?" I laughed.

"Cottage Cat-aclysm," she countered.

"I like that one." I hugged her good morning.

She held a big coffee mug close to her chest. With mussed hair and dark circles under her eyes, she looked like a waif from *Les Miserables*. Her bedroom was next to mine on the second floor. I knew she'd been sleeping, from the snoring I heard, but it was obviously not restful.

"Laura and I will be taking our leave from the Hilltop Hotel today," Claire stated. "If you don't mind, I'll leave Mutt here until I get the house straightened up."

"Fine, but you gals have only been here four days. Why are you rushing off? Our cuisine not up to your standards?" I asked.

"Not a thing wrong with kitty kibbles in my book," she snickered. "Roasted, baked, boiled . . ."

Brushing the cobwebs and dust from my hands, I stood there mesmerized by the mess. "This was going to be the parlor. There's a fireplace over there behind those boxes. Remember?"

She glanced at the old stuff. "It wouldn't take much to fix this place up," she said without criticism in her voice.

I nodded. "Nothing but money, will, and energy. All of which I decidedly lack these days."

"When you don't have strength in yourself, find strength in your friends."

"You are truth, herself," I said opening a box of pictures.

The one on top was of Doc and me on a picnic with Claire and whomever she was dating at the time. She sat in the background laughing so hard she cried. I was attempting to do a cartwheel and Doc held me upside down. It looked like he was getting ready to break a wishbone. I smiled and showed it to her before I closed the box back up.

"We had some good times," she acknowledged.

"Yes, we did." I managed to say without adding any negativity.

"The biohazard crew didn't take as long as I thought they would. There wasn't a lot for them to take out at my house. Not like . . ."

She must have been remembering the major reconstruction I had to do at the condo before I sold it. No one wanted to buy it with an eight-foot hole in the second floor.

"Anyway, my new carpet should be installed by this afternoon."

"Color?" I asked.

"A bluish-green. Same color as the sea in the Caribbean."

"Nice. That will suit you. You and Laura don't have to leave so quickly. I mean a body in your closet is not what worries me as much as the realization that someone put him there, and that someone could still be running the streets of Angel Falls. No disrespect meant to JD, my concern is for you and Laura."

I judiciously avoided the words "set-up, scapegoat, unknown enemy," and "tag-team serial killers." Claire didn't respond. She looked past me doing a good impersonation of the hundred-yard stare. I couldn't read her features.

Does she daydream of tranquil turquoise waters or pirates?

"What are you thinking about?" I ventured.

"Many things, my friend, many things great and small. I'm at one of those special moments in my life. If I still lived in Florida, I'd pull anchor and sail down to the next key, but I'm not near enough to the open sea to run away."

"Leave?" I squeaked. My stomach lurched when I remembered the "For Sale" sign in her front window.

Claire continued, "I don't deal with ghosts as well as you do." She patted my hand and wandered off to finish her coffee in privacy.

It occurred to me that the focus of these murder investigations was changing from "what and where" they happened, into "who" they happened to. Were these events about Jimmy and JD, or were they about my best friend, Claire? Locks on doors were easier to break than locks on hearts. After Doc died, my heart got vaulted.

When I walked out of the front room Harv stopped fiddling with the deadbolt. He must have heard Ross's admonition. Harvey replaced the locks on all our doors, and fixed the window latches that afternoon. He did the same at Claire's house, and in Laura's garage apartment. Then he cautioned us to start using the latches with a severity that would have made Ross proud.

#

Harvey got on a home-improvement kick after changing the locks. He repaired the hole in our roof. He replaced boards on the external and internal stairways to the second and third floors, making them usable for human and cat alike. He reinforced the railing all around the party terrace. He pulled the old shutters out from our storage shed, and restored the missing slats. Except for new paint, the outside of the house had been brought up to code.

I wanted to paint the house purple, but Harvey threatened to move out. We settled on a light grey base to compliment the darker grey shingles. Then we used white and dark purple on the trim around the windows and the accent pieces. Harvey hoped the purple would look dark grey from the road.

A man's got to have his fantasies.

Murder and my own mental mayhem kept me awake at nights. During the witching hour I prowled the newly painted party terrace, full goblet in hand with Max and Cricket in tow.

Harvey no longer worried about me plunging to my death accidentally or on purpose. Punkin still didn't like the wind on the third level, choosing instead to warm my pillows as she waited, ever patient, in my bedroom for my return.

The view from the third floor is worth the climb.

The scene down into our little hamlet from the party terrace amazed me. This high up, I could see the whole town. The last two houses on the main street faded into darkness, but our five streetlights along with business signs and porch lights lit the rest of town in a soft glow. Angel Falls was growing towards the north. I had visions of housing developments and shopping malls to come.

Dare I hope for a multi-plex cinema?

During my midnight strolls I sought reasons for the two deaths, rather than accept some random acts of violence, but connecting the threads and threats lay beyond my addled mind, wine soaked or sober.

Where is Gary Sinise and his CSI: NY team when you need them?

Daily, I did the insane sleuth two-step: looking for clues, not seeing clues right in front of me, uncovering tidbits of information, not knowing how to weave them into coherent meaning. I treaded emotional and intellectual water, not moving in any direction.

In real life, nothing happens for long periods of time.

And nothing happened in Angel Falls for a few weeks. Life continued into the beginnings of tourist season without incident, but not without rumor. Claire's Bar and Grill buzzed with business. I started helping out on Saturday nights, not as a psychic, but as an extra waitress. Glen, the new cook, was incredible. The food went from so-so to spectacular. Laura designed a menu for the fresh cuisine, and street chatter named Claire's as "The Place to Be." Actually, everyone started calling it, Carill's. When Claire turned on the neon sign for the season only the C, a, r, i, l, l lit up.

I knew superstition said it was bad luck to change the name of a boat, but this change felt like the right thing to do.

The burger and fries remained, but tasty American and Italian dishes, a Catch of the Day and a weekly Chef's Surprise took focus. Glen created his "surprise" dishes like a cooking show challenge. Customers could bring in any two cans of food from their pantry: one went to the local food bank and the second got plated in a chef's prerogative dish created expressly for the givers.

Don't ask about the white chocolate drizzled asparagus.

Carill's served up lunch and dinner in real dishes, on real

tablecloths -- no more plastic plates and butcher paper disposable covers for this establishment. No smoking and no pool playing were probably next, but not this season. Angel Falls eased rather than jumped into change.

The town filled with new and familiar faces excited about vacations yet to come. The vet clinic went through a birthing blitz with only one casualty. I didn't have time to get back to the courthouse to do more digging, but the Internet and I became midnight e-pals. I didn't tell anyone what I found, yet. Not even Harvey or Claire. My sin of omission was intentional. Pieces to the puzzle were missing. I already had the reputation of being two steps to the left of center. I wanted my speculations to have merit and factual substance, when I got ready to share them.

#

Since JD had no known family members, after the sheriff's department went through his belongings, Claire got them. There wasn't a lot to show for his life: one duffel bag of clothing, a golf umbrella, and a plastic sack of groceries he had apparently pilfered from her kitchen. It made me sad. Claire took most of his stuff down to the church shelter. She told me she kept a Harley tee shirt, his toothbrush and a hat.

Far be it for me to question someone's choice in

memorabilia.

Claire seemed fine. I guessed for her, gone really meant gone. I preferred more drawn out, torturous good-byes. Along with Doc's household items packed up in my parlor, I had a suitcase full of his clothes in the top of my closet. His scent had worn off years ago, both living and dead, replaced by my snot and tears. Tomorrow the shelter would get another donation.

Accepting the things I cannot change instead of slamming my head against a wall. What a novel concept?

Claire and I decided before it got more crowded or crazed in town we should set a time for the long overdue memorial service. We hadn't forgotten about honoring Jimmy. The needs of everyday living took precedence over the God-Bye-Ye Ceremony. We made it a "two-for" and added JD's name to the back of the Serenity Prayer bookmark keepsake. I printed twenty-five at the CopyQuick, the same place I'd copied Jimmy's photos only two months ago.

My days walk into weeks, sometimes without me noticing. The day/date wall clock Doc gave me comes in handy if I have to figure out "when" I am.

We scheduled the gathering for a slow Tuesday. Claire put a "Private Party" sign on the front doors. The locals understood. The tourists respected the notice and took their libations elsewhere for the afternoon. We wanted to celebrate Jimmy and JD's lives. We wanted music on the jukebox, cheers going up, funny stories being told, and beers being consumed. Lots of beers.

Okay, I want that for my wake.

Since the guys both died under tragic and suspicious circumstances, Claire felt we should downplay the celebration aspect. We displayed a five by seven picture of Jimmy on the bar next to a cold basket of curly fries, and his old Mobil baseball cap. We placed a smaller photo of JD on the other side of the potatoes. Laura put candles along the bar, and I brought a bouquet of flowers and herbs from my garden.

"Where did you find Jimmy's hat?" I asked Claire.

"It's not Jimmy's," Claire answered. "I found it in JD's duffel."

"Look at it. This is exactly like the one Jimmy came back to get the night he disappeared. And exactly like the one Ross said he saw in his cousin Joe's trailer."

"Now that you mention it." Claire picked the hat up and put it on her head. It fit. "Damn, girlfriend. This snap-cap is set too small for JD's big ol' head."

"And you *found* it in JD's duffel?

"Yes, Nan. In a side pocket."

I snatched it off her head and stashed it under the counter.

"Watch the hair," she rebuked me.

"One ratty-tatty, flying horse baseball cap gone missing is nothing to fret over, but having the same flying horse hat pop back up at Jimmy's cousin's house, and again in JD's belongings?"

"Put a dish towel over it!" Claire blurted as if it were an evil artifact to be contained by dirty cotton. "I don't want your cousin to see it."

We realized it at the same moment. Ross already had seen it. We said, "Shit," in tandem. I pulled the cap back out, brushed off a flake of dried food.

"Guess there's no sense in hiding it," I muttered. "Hell, Ross probably put it in the duffel." I checked inside to see if a treasure map stuck inside the brim. No such luck. It occurred to me that I should watch people's reactions to the hat when they passed by to pay their respects. I set it in between the two pictures.

The *Usual Suspects* came and went during the open house memorial service with a few individuals I didn't know dropping in to say goodbye. An elderly lady sat in one of the booths but didn't socialize with anyone. A couple of guys I assumed were from Jimmy's high school raised a toast in his honor, while other folks came in, looked at the pictures, dropped a dollar in the donation jar and left. Claire, Laura, and I decided to donate a book in Jimmy's memory to the library in Zoerne. Angel Falls got regular visits from the Zoerne Public Library Book-mobile. We thought it fitting. We were in debate as to whether the book should be a young adult novel, a cookbook, or a murder-mystery contribution. If we collected enough money we'd put a nameplate in a book for JD too.

When the crowd faded to the final few, Claire told everyone how she had met JD at Jimmy's gas station. JD changed her tire while Jimmy tinkered with someone's timing belt.

"I told him if he was as handy in a kitchen as in a garage I'd hire him. He was, and I did." Claire raised her shot of Crown. "To JD."

"To JD," we responded.

One of the younger townsfolk, his name escaped me, told a story of how Jimmy got lost in the woods when he was little, and slept all night in the hollow of a tree. He went on to say it was Joe who found Jimmy.

"Joe knew right where to look for him," the young man said.

An uncomfortable idea lodged in my head. Had Joe found Jimmy with tracking skill? By luck? Or because he left the boy by the tree in the first place?

"We miss you, Jim," his friend said and swallowed the last of his beer.

We all followed suit. We didn't have a minister, and we didn't say a prayer. Laura got up after the last toast and played Marie Osmond's "Pie Jesu" on her iPhone. Marie sang the opera aria in memory of her late son. Her clear, soprano voice filled the silent room, enchanting, even on one speaker. I wasn't the only person wiping my eyes after the song.

It was done. Folks drifted out the door, some said "thank you" to Claire for hosting the service. Snookie came over and hugged both Claire and me before she left. I helped Laura clean while Claire packed up the pictures and candles. She left the hat out. The afternoon disappointed me on two accounts. No one but Claire raised a tribute to JD. And, Joe and Jerri Ann did not bother to come. Ross showed up as we wrapped the wake. He tossed five dollars in the book donation bowl.

"Well?" he asked.

"Well, what?" I responded.

"What, how?" he continued.

"How, who?" I said back to him in a word game we'd

played since childhood. The first one to drop the questions lost the game.

"Who, exactly," Ross chose to lose.

"You scoundrel. You planted that baseball cap," I accused him.

"Did anyone react to it?" Ross asked unabashed. "Did you get any odd feelings?"

"No and no. And where were you this afternoon?"

"Outside watching, taking notes on who showed up," Ross said.

Claire walked up beside me. I put my arm around her.

"And on who didn't make an appearance," Claire said with a touch of resentment creeping into her voice.

"Yeah, that too," admitted Ross.

"You off duty?" she asked him.

"I am now."

Claire walked behind the bar and pulled out three more longnecks. "From here on, we're toasting the living," she announced.

We clinked bottles.

Death By Catgut

Pause For Paws

Harvey couldn't get off work for the memorial service. He was working a bunch of extra hours. This time of year the store geared up for the influx of travelers and the increase in tourist trade. Harv sent a donation for the book, and condolences through me. I didn't hold his absence against him, but I worried about him. Since I'd passed my expiration date he'd been acting different.

Claire declined an invite to Hilltop for dinner after the service, but the Ross followed me home. After beer and several helpings of curly fries at the B & G, I could feel my arteries clogging shut. I planned to toss some green things in a bowl, threaten the lettuce with cheese and pour any dressing we had in the fridge on top.

To my surprise when my cousin and I arrived, my housemate had dinner waiting to be plated: pot roast, potatoes, carrots, onions and gravy. Harvey heard us come in and was adding a plate to the table when Ross begged a rain check.

"That aroma's making my stomach growl, but thanks all the same, Harv. My better half is expecting me to put my cowboy boots under her table tonight."

"Forgot the wine!" Harvey headed back into the kitchen.

Ross wiggled his eyebrows at me and mouthed, "You and Harvey getting cozy?"

"Yew, no. That would be like doing you," I defended my honor in a whisper.

"Like doing me . . . yew," my cousin repeated.

I whapped him on the shoulder. He pretended to be affronted by the entire matter.

"Hey, that's assaulting an officer of the law."

"You're off duty."

When it became obvious that Ross and I were not going to talk any more this evening, he made his goodbyes. But something was definitely up with Harvey. His house-fixing frenzy freaked me out. He stopped short of landscaping on the outside and directed his efforts inside. The boxes and furniture had been moved from the parlor. Harv didn't tell me where he stored all that old stuff, and I didn't really care. The cache of other people's belongings began when I got Mom and Doc's leftover households, then Harvey got his sister's things, my brother Zach stored a few things at our place, etc., etc., etc. My philosophy was if I hadn't worn an outfit or used a household utensil in three years, chances were I didn't really need it, but I had inherited the packrat gene. Things accumulated in spite of me.

Sheetrock wall panels stood in the corner of the soon-to-be living room along with lumber. Harvey stacked carpet samples and several gallons of butter cream yellow paint alongside the rest. I told my housemate the colors I preferred for inside when we painted the outside of the house. And he had listened.

After a couple of false starts and one accidental full body spraying, I got a handle on how to use the paint gun. I did not see Harvey behind the shutters -- that's my story. The grass would recover with watering, and we were done painting in four and a half days . . . the whole house.

I sat at the table and unfolded my paper napkin. Harvey had taken an empty paint can and put some flowers in it. He had mad cooking skills, but he didn't take the time to prepare a whole meal often. We ate a lot of Grab-N-Go or microwave mania.

"Nan, I've got things I need to talk to you about," he

said.

Harvey poured me a glass of wine from a bottle instead of a box. It had a pretty label. I started bawling, big, stupid, crocodile tears and gave myself an immediate case of the hiccups.

"You're moving out to go back to school!" I blurted out between the hic and the cup.

"What?" Harvey looked genuinely confused.

He thought I was choking. He walked over to my chair and pounded me on the back.

"Not helping." Hiccup, sob, burp. *Damn it. If I keep this up I'm going to pee on myself.* "Please stop pounding me on the back."

"Sorry?" he made it sound like a question.

I gulped down my wine. That stopped the hiccups, but I didn't get to appreciate the bouquet until a second glass of the expensive Merlot. I blew my nose as gracefully as I could on my paper napkin, took a breath and tried to wait out the silence.

"You okay?" he asked.

"Yes. I'm sorry, Harvey. Dinner is lovely. Thank you. Pass the carrots, please."

He did.

"Nan?"

"Yes."

"Would you mind if I asked Claire out on a date?"

This time I snorted Merlot through my nose. I avoided ruining my plate by gagging to the side. I sprayed Snowball in burgundy liquid. Of all our cats, it had to be the white one. She looked like a full moon sacrifice. Harvey had a moment of hesitation, then did what I would have, ignored me and grabbed a towel to clean off the cat. Snowball dried to a softer shade of pink. I reeled in enough air to speak.

"Why?"

"Because I like her."

"No. Why ask me, if you can ask her?" I asked him.

Harvey put the cat and towel down, brushed the cat hair from his hands and sat back down at the table. During the long pause, I ate my carrots. I was going to win this round of waiting.

"Because you are our best friend. You're my best friend, and you're Claire's best friend. I don't want to put you in an awkward position if the relationship goes sideways."

My knee-jerk reaction was anger. "If you don't want to put me in an awkward situation, don't put me in an awkward situation. Sideways? Ya-think? You've hung around Claire for more than twenty years, and never once crossed that line. Why now, Harvey? Why?"

"I told you I was ready for my life to move in a new direction. I think she might be it. I've always ..." He struggled to find a middle-age appropriate word. "I've always *fancied* her, but this is the first time in our lives when we've both single at the same time."

I paused, and realized Harvey had put thought into this. I smashed a well into my potatoes, and reached for the gravy. "The last time I did your laundry, there were big boy briefs in the load. You don't need my permission."

"Yes, I do."

"I thought you were going back to school," I said.

"I am. I've got to pick up some refresher courses this summer. I plan to go back full-time in the fall, but I'm not leaving you. I'm not moving out. What makes you say that?"

"All this!" I pointed to the renovations in progress. "Why are you fixing up the house? Where did you get the money to go back to school? And you want to date Claire? You know, she's not a cheap date."

That made him laugh.

"We've been living here for the past five years on the cheap. I thought you needed the sameness in your surroundings to save your sanity with everything you were going through. I've been putting money in a savings account, and I took a chunk of the money I got from my sister's life insurance and invested well. It's time to stop living in the shambles. All the crap happening in Angel Falls made me realize how quickly our best-made plans alter, even if we don't want them to." He took a swallow of wine. "Nan, I want my life to change, and I want you to be okay with it."

"Tired of Nan duty?"

Harvey came over and knelt beside me. He took my hands in his.

"You were, are, and always will be my best, best friend. I'm not your father. I'm not your brother. I'm not your lover or looking to be, so I can say this with certainty: as long as I am alive I will be here for you." He moved one of my hands over his heart and pressed it into his chest.

There it was, his simple declaration: "I love you," without saying the words and with no conditions. I didn't cry. My mind changed into slow motion. What a collection of emotions swept through me: fear, anger, resentment, then acceptance and joy. The last two I had neglected to feel for a long, long time. I leaned over and kissed his forehead.

"I love you, too," I whispered into his hair. "And now it's time for you to focus on you." I pulled him up into a hug then pushed him off. "Fine! Run off and get educated, date my best friend, but you better have one hellofa great dessert waiting behind door number three because after all this, I need sugar."

We finished dinner with only small talk. The fur children anxiously waited for their share of the gravy. Harvey made the meat sauce without garlic or onion salt. That way the kitties could have their share. I promised to do the dishes in the morning, but begged off cleanup duties this evening. A wash of fatigue overtook me. I wanted to lie down before I fell down in front of Harvey. The only way to relieve him of Nan duty was to take care of myself.

#

I felt no stab of pain. I saw no blinding flashes of light. I wore red chiffon. A train of flowing material trailed behind me and pooled around my feet like stilled water.

Or was it drying blood?

The moon's shrouded halo cast down a burgundy light on a cloudless night. A white cat sat in the corner of our party patio wearing a red cape. My calico locks blew around me in an Animae heroine's windstorm hairdo. I floated to the top of our roof, and balanced on the rooster weathervane.

We need to replace that rooster with a cat theme.

I peered down into Angel Falls peacefully asleep. Indignation grew inside me. How dared they all rest when two souls were lost under our watch? Lightning shot from my fingertips and struck the gas station's neon sign. Jimmy and JD stood nearby, half in shadows. They did a full court bow in my direction. Caught in the light from the bolt of lightning, and the neon sign flash, their eyes glowed up at me like my cats in the dark. I laughed like a mad woman. I mean really laughed, loud enough to wake myself up.

Some warrior goddess I am.

Downstairs held the promise of a different kind of sanguine fluid. Sweet, red box-o-wine called my name. Held in the illusion (or delusion) of my dream, I swirled into our newly painted kitchen in my Yoyo and Hoops house shoes. Not exactly the vision of my dreams. I poured myself a large goblet and plopped in a couple of ice cubes. I never succumbed to my baser wine tastes in public, but in my own home, at four in the morning, with no one watching, two ice cubes weren't going to insult anyone's fine dinning acumen.

I wondered why Jimmy and JD were at the gas station. My visions weren't always easy to figure out. Fidget glanced up at me with his sleepy face from his spot on the table. He seemed to say, "It's too late for last call, and too early for breakfast. What's up?"

Why were Jimmy and JD together in my dream? I sipped

251

my wine, and remembered that Claire mentioned she met JD at the gas station. What was he doing there besides changing her tire and setting up his next meal ticket? I played my dream over in my mind. They stood in half-light, side by side. They raised their faces up to me before they bowed. I saw it.

Crap, crap, crap.

Jimmy and JD had the same color eyes. That would not be noticing much if they had average brown, or blue, or green, or even grey ones. No, no, no, both men's eyes were honey-amber with a chocolate ring around the outside of the iris, feral in some light. And come to think of it, so did Joe. This called for a second glass of wine. I chugged my first one. Fidget put his paw on my arm and I paused. As a comfort cat in training, his touch meant I needed to listen to him. I poured myself a glass of water instead and pondered my dream.

Genetics being what they were, I guessed the three "J"s were related. Well, duh. Jimmy and Joe were cousins. Where did JD fit in? My Internet research revealed that Gramps Jackson had two sons. And Bobby, our pizza-guy, had mentioned that Joe and his mother left Angel Falls shortly after his father went missing. Or went off on his own accord to places unknown. JD was older than Jimmy and Joe, but probably not as old as me. It was difficult for me to figure age. He was in good shape, but had spent too much time in the sun unprotected. Claire was five years my junior, but she never labeled her lovers by birthdates. My estimate put JD at forty-five to fifty. Splitting the difference, forty-seven would make him the right age to be Gramps Jackson's missing son: Jimmy's uncle and Joe's long lost dad.

Tail Tale Signs

I showed up at the sheriff's department after my work.

"You playing with those papers?" I asked my cousin.

"It's called filing. I would have thought you'd heard of it, seeing as you work in an office," Ross barked back at me.

"I have more important duties."

"Yeah, like cleaning up the duty." He mimicked pushing a broom across the floor, "What? And give up show business?"

"Hey now, be nice, or I won't share my dream with you."

"Oh joy of joys. I can hardly wait," Ross sniped.

"Wow, who pissed in your Wheaties this morning?"

Ross let out a deep sigh, and ran his fingers over his new spring buzz cut. "Sorry darling, long day."

He came around the desk, and made to bear hug me. I didn't know if I should run or endure the squeeze. I choose the latter.

"So, can you talk about what's got you grumpy?" I asked. "You don't do grumpy with any style. You may have to take some lessons from me."

That remark made him smile. He waved his hands around to indicate his whole office, but stopped to rub his chest.

"Spill it," I demanded.

"Everything and nothing."

"Wow. You really do sound like me. Cuz, that is not a compliment."

"It is more than you know."

Ross reached into his desk drawer and pulled out a bottle of bourbon. He poured me two fingers and slid the tin cup across his desk.

"You not partaking?" I asked.

"Drinking doesn't help me like it does you. The alcohol doesn't clarify my mind's eye, or dull the pain. Lately, all it does is add to my heartburn."

"Sorry to hear that."

Ross snorted, "What the hell." Before he stoppered the bottle he took a long swig.

"Where's your deputy?"

"He's out cruising the county. Ronnie's a good man. He'll be a good sheriff," Ross speculated.

"We've got a good sheriff," I said.

"Not after this term. Come elections, I'm done."

I sat stunned. I chugged my glass and reached for his bottle.

"I don't want to do this anymore," my cousin admitted.

"Do what?" I pretended not to understand.

"I've already talked it over with my family, and I'm not going to run for sheriff when my term ends."

I could hear the hum of the florescent lights in the silence. The room smelled like lemon Pledge. Everything narrowed down to a pinprick of light.

#

I found myself in a graveyard, again. It took me a moment to remember which one. Ross stood beside me as we peered down into my father's open grave. It looked like a bottomless pit to me then and now. I held a rose from the casket spray in my left hand so tightly the thorns bled me. There were four small piles of dirt on the coffin from my mother and my brothers. I was last in line. I couldn't do it. I couldn't let the dirt go. Ross took my right hand, gently pried open my little girl fingers, and brushed the soil from my palm.

In Zoëtrophic horror, every funeral and open grave I'd ever stood before flashed through my mind in sepia-colored shadows ending with three urns of ash sitting on a red brick fence labeled: Jimmy, JD and Nan.

Ashes, ashes, we all fall down.

#

"Say something," Ross demanded.

"Okay?" I furrowed my brows. Ross was wrapped up in his own agenda and missed my mini-time travelling episode. I covered my lapse with, "What's the right response? Why? Why leave this job? You were a hall monitor when you were twelve. You're good at this, and God knows this piss-poor town needs you."

Ross fidgeted with pushpins on the county road map. "Back in the day, they used urine to tan hides? Some people sold their pee when they needed money. That's where the term 'piss poor' comes from."

"How much of this bottle did you have before I got here?"

"Medicinal purposes only."

I could tell he struggled. I toned down my teasing. "History lesson aside, what brought all this up?"

"If I say I'm done, it sounds like I'm quitting. I'm not quitting. It's not because I can't handle the pressure of the two murders . . . The bottom line is I'm ready for a change."

257

"There's a lot of that going around," I mumbled into my second drink. "What are you going to do?"

"I don't know, but I've got the better part of a year to figure it out. In the meantime, what can I do for you?"

"If I said: feral amber eyes, three 'J's, open graves, bloody hands, and I'm next, would that collection of totally unrelated items make any sense to you?"

"As the sheriff, no. As your cousin and the grandson of Winifred Dorkus Cude-Atkins, maybe. I need more info to play connect-the-dots."

"Did you run DNA, fingerprints, background stuff on JD?"

"Yeah. There was nothing on him in the system."

"If he was ex-military, like he told Claire, there'd be a paper trail. You found nothing?"

"Nothing real."

"Nowadays it's almost impossible to be invisible. Even if somebody doesn't have credit cards, there's driver's licenses, social security cards, cell phones . . . geez Ross, all you've got to do is FaceBook, FaceTime, Google, Bing, Bang, Boom, Match Dot anyone to find your long lost love, family, friend. Hell, there's even a Stalker.com. You can damn-near find out what people eat for breakfast, where they shop, and when they have a bowel movement. It's scary."

Ross suppressed a snicker. "The fact that you are actually using computer terms is what's scary."

"I can go home." I got up to leave.

"Naw, Nannie, I'm teasing you. Sit back down. Where are you going with all of this?"

"JD, as we knew him, didn't exist. What was Jimmy's uncle called?"

He sucked air through his teeth as he thought. "That was a long time ago. Jonathan, Josiah, maybe. The whole family's first names began with 'J's. I can look him up. Why?"

"And they all have amber eyes that catch a feral, honey glow in certain light. I think JD was Joe's long lost daddy. Claire said she met him at the gas station. What if he was at the station remaking his acquaintance with his nephew? What if JD asked about his share of Gramps Jackson's money? What if Joe found out JD was his dad? Can you say 'awkward family reunion'?"

"There's a lot of 'what ifs' in your thinking." Ross started pacing.

He didn't dismiss my conjectures. And, he didn't believe I was crazy. I loved him for that. I wondered if he'd felt anything surging through our shared wild blood and bond?

"You got any hunches about all this . . . off the record?" I asked him.

"Is Schrodinger cat alive or dead?"

"Hah, I got this one. I watch *Big Bang Theory*. It's Quantum Physics." I lifted a finger to keep him from interrupting. I didn't get the chance to be clever often. "All possibilities exist at the same time, until the artifact or moment in question is viewed. Then, by the very act of being observed, the reality in question is fixed. So, JD is all things at this moment."

Ross gave me a golf clap. "If Joe is related to JD that bumps him and Jerri Ann up on the suspect list. They alibied each other for the night of Jimmy's death. I wonder what they will say about JD?"

"Nobody can piss us off like family." I feigned innocence when my cousin started nodding like a martyr. "But Ross, if my father showed up after twenty-five years I'd be mad, but not mad enough to kill him."

"If your dad showed up, in the flesh, you ought to be scared. He died when we were ten."

I started to throw the tin cup at him, but it had a swallow of bourbon left in it. "Fine. Why kill your cousin?"

To his credit, Ross didn't make a sarcastic remark at my

expense. "Money's always a motive."

I told him what I'd found in the archives at the county courthouse.

"Sounds like the land title slipped through the cracks. Some of those old deeds never got transferred onto the computer system. If the gas station is still in Gramps Jackson's name, with no will or binding accord in place, it would go first to his spouse, then to his sons, then to his grandsons."

"It sort of did, but it went to the seconds, the second born son and the second born grandson," I said.

"JD lived here for what five months? That's a lot of time wasted on cooking up curly fries if his reason for being here was to claim his part of the gas station."

"Maybe he wanted to check out everything and everyone before he took action. He left Angel Falls a long time ago."

"Could be," Ross speculated.

"Claire kept JD's toothbrush if you need his DNA. If she didn't clean her toilet with it," I snorted.

"What a lovely, feminine sound," Ross teased.

That made me laugh more and I snorted again. "You're lucky it's a snort, not a . . ."

"Hey now. Thank you, but we've got DNA from Jimmy and JD on record. I can have the lab check them against each other. That info won't be back for a couple of weeks. I can ask Joe to volunteer a cheek swab, but if he's had anything to do with this mess he'll decline."

"Can you force him?" I asked.

"Not without probable cause and a court order."

"What you're telling me is we're still guessing if the cat in the box is dead or alive."

"Pretty much, yes." Ross sat at his desk and opened a file folder. I tried to glance over the top. He slammed it down on top of several others and swore. From the look on his face I could tell he'd made up his mind about something, but didn't like it.

"Anything I can do to help?" I offered.

"You up for some she-Nan-igans?" he asked me.

I arched my brows. "Always."

"I think you need to do one of your card readings for Joe."

"Joe's never been in, but I've done a couple for Jerri Ann."

"Might work."

"Let me guess, you want me to stack the deck."

#

Turning the ignition key in old Betsy Mae was a practice

in wish fulfillment and disappointment. Harvey helped me push the VW Bug to the edge of the driveway. I hoped the downward momentum would be enough for the car to turn over. I headed to Jackson's Gas-N-Go to get the oil changed. While I waited, I planned to make small talk with Joe's current girlfriend.

Jerri Ann sported a new striped hairdo, a new spandex outfit, new high-heeled ankle boots, along with a new set of acrylic nails too long and too red to be tasteful. She had on the diamond earrings and necklace she started wearing after Joe took over the gas station. I chose to comment on the shoes.

"Great platforms. Bedazzled retro or new spikey vanguard?"

"Painful Internet purchase," said Jerri Ann.

"Buyers remorse?"

"Not really. I wish I had Band-Aids with me. I can't pull any off the shelf unless I pay for them." She made a disgusted sound through her nose. "When Joey said 'we' would run the station, I didn't realize he meant 'me.' I work in here all day while he sits in the garage reading magazines waiting for someone to drive in and pump their own gas."

High heels can make a woman cranky.

"You want to wear my flip-flops?" I wiggled my toes at her.

Jerri Ann grimaced, as politely as she could. "I think your feet are too little."

"Suit yourself. I brought my old bug in for an oil change."

Jerri Ann "um-hummed" me, and went back to rearranging the stack of miniature pecan pies. "Oh, help yourself to free coffee. I'm supposed to offer our clientele coffee."

"Thanks."

I poured a cup and sat in one of the three folding chairs. After a bit, began to shuffle my cards. The soft ruffling sound, soothing to me, acted like a magnet. Jerri Ann began to circle closer and closer.

"If you give me one of those pecan pies to wash down this coffee, I'll do a reading for you," I offered.

She turned her back on me, and fluffed up the Frito-Lay bags. "I have work to do."

"Suit yourself. I thought it would pass the time."

She moved so fast, I considered she might have super powers. She must be bored out of her mind. Jimmy seemed to like all the quiet, but I'd go crazy in this gas-station-grocery-nic-nac prison too.

"I'm supposed to make the customers happy."

Jerri Ann pulled the two other folding chairs in front of

me. She sat down in one, and we use the third as a table. She offered up my pecan pie.

"What are you up for today?" I asked. "Five Card Stud? Jacks are wild?" I teased. Her blank expression let me know she didn't get my humor. I moved on. "Well, there really isn't enough room to do a normal card layout. How about I do a Life Castle for you?"

"What's a Life Castle?"

"I don't do a reading like this often because it takes a lot of energy out of me." I totally pulled that out of my ass. "We will build a house of cards as I lay them out for you."

Her mouth made a small "O," and I knew I had her.

"Cut the deck, and let's see what the Powers That Be have to tell you."

I'd been working with cards most of my life. I could pull off a few sleight of hand tricks that would make a street magician proud. When Jerri Ann cut the deck, I made two quick flips, and had the cards stacked the way I wanted. The key to getting away with a lie is consistency with enough truth sprinkled in to make it believable. Doc taught me that. If you say it often enough, everyone will believe you. Sometimes you can even convince yourself.

Catastrophe

"This first card is your present situation." I said as I flipped over the dragon card for Strength. I put it in the center of the plastic chair between us. I didn't know if I felt like an amateur sleuth or charlatan card shark. I'd never purposefully distorted anyone's reading before. "This card is your foundation."

Jerri Ann smiled at the idea of being strong. She wasn't the brightest candle in the chandelier. I knew I could make her believe any thing I wanted her to. Playing an emotional Svengali didn't feel good, but I continued.

"The next three cards are walls in your castle. The first points to your past, the second to your present, the third to your future." I lay them out flat first to view whether they were upright or downward.

"The Chariot is in a negative position," I said.

Jerri Ann frowned and shifted in her chair.

"Wait. Upside down is not a bad thing here," I encouraged. I didn't want her to leave before I got started. "It means that your life was not going in the direction you wanted it to."

She relaxed.

"This next card, "your present" shows that you are self-reliant. It also tells me that you are struggling with . . ." I pretended to search for the correct words. "You are struggling with an event. Did something happen to upset you, dear?"

Jerri Ann touched her new diamond necklace, unconscious of her gesture. I patted her knee. I didn't want to push too far, too fast.

"There, there, it's been an odd spring around here. Let's look to your future." I turned over the third card, and made my ever-so-concerned face. "The Emperor. This card is upside-down too. It means someone near you is untrustworthy." I inclined my head toward the garage, but I should have pointed the finger at myself.

Would The Mentalist say I set up the mark?

"The first floor of your castle is more about outside influences." I made the three cards into a triangle. "The second story is more about you."

The Lovers showed up next. I had Jerri Ann place the

card on top of the triangle as a floorboard. She managed not to knock it all over. We were building a house of cards on a folding chair, for goodness sake.

"Love is your internal foundation."

Since I was making this up as I went along, I had no idea how to balance another level of cards, but we managed to construct a second floor to her card castle while I prattled on.

"This card shows you are a strong woman capable of leadership, and the Hanging Dragon," I pointed to the green wyvern hanging by his feet. "This tells me you are ready to move on with your life. I have some concerns about the Temperance card for your personal future . . . It indicates you are overwhelmed." I paused with a pained furrow on my brow. "There may be a rival."

Jerri Ann shifted in her folding chair.

"The next layer in your castle is simple. The foundation card represents your deepest desires. On top of that rather than three cards, there will only be two. Kind of like the spires on a castle rampart." I steepled my fingers and gave her a visual clue. "The first card will be obstacles you may face, the second card will give you guidance."

She paled when I flipped up the Death Dragon for the floor. I continued to turn over the Wheel of Fate and the

Judgment Dragon. I acted shocked.

"Let's stack these up and look at the Ultimate Outcome card. Imagine it is a flag flying from the highest bastion . . . wall from your castle. All this may make perfect sense with the last card," I encouraged.

Jerri Ann didn't move. She stared at the cards while I set up the final pinnacle. As I started to show her the last card, Joe opened the side door. The wind from his entrance scattered the castle. He stood trying to fill as much of the doorframe as possible. He combed a stray strand of hair away from his eyes with a blue-green pocket comb, cocksure in a menacing way.

I whispered loud enough for only Jerri Ann to hear, "Catastrophe."

"Oh, Joe. Look what you've done!" She stood and shook a finger at him. "She can't finish my reading."

"You've got work to do," Joe scolded.

"I am working," she sassed back. "Customer service."

Wow. She has spunk if not spark.

"Your car is ready, Witch." Joe's aggravation turned to me.

"That's Miss Witch, to you Joseph. I'm old enough to be your . . . Auntie. Show me respect, or I'll pull your ear and hang chicken feet over your door."

He actually looked chagrinned, tipped an imaginary hat at me and ducked back out to the garage.

I hope he's not putting sugar in my gas tank.

Jerri Ann handed me my cards. "I'll send you the bill. You better go."

I grabbed her in a fierce hug. "You take care of yourself. We've had two murders in this town in two months. Don't make it three in three."

Damn threes.

Tears formed in the corner of her eyes. I made a quick exit. I didn't know what made me say that. I needed a shower. I felt dirty, and it wasn't from being in the garage.

#

Sleuthing seemed easy for Jessica Fletcher in *Murder, She Wrote.* A murder, a mystery, a motive, then the bad guys got caught and hauled off to jail. Things fell in a different order, here. I had a full case of what Harvey called the whim-whams by the time I got home. I'd gone to the garage with the intention of pulling information out of Jerri Ann vis-a-vis me inserting seeds of doubt and veiled accusations in her card reading.

Granny Winnie, forgive me.

I made up the whole "Castle" schtick, but the more I thought about it, the more the reading felt true. It didn't matter how I spread or stacked the cards, the message felt as accurate as any other, including the warning for her to be careful.

Ross would say we needed proof. The only proof I had on my mind after escaping the garage was 16% liqueur, a passion fruit, cherry, and ginger blend imported from France called Alisé.

Alisé in Wonderland? Won't be the first time I explore a rabbit hole.

I needed to put on my witchy paraphernalia and head for my Friday night gig at Carill's. Claire was too busy for our traditional greeting when I swirled in, but I got applause from Laura as I flapped my sequin encrusted, gauze-wing sleeves. I stopped in mid-flight. The most wonderful aroma floated through the B & G. Laura walked past me and pushed my mouth shut.

"Friday is Italian night," she explained.

"OMG. I think I put on five pounds from the smell alone."

"The lasagna is to die for." Laura's eyes went dark for a moment. "I mean . . ."

I waved her off before she got stuck in the shadows. "Smuggle me a chunk, you wicked waitress."

The place was packed, due in no short order to Glen's

271

new menu and cooking ability. Plus the tourist traffic continued to increase. Laura had talked Judy and me into changing our rates and set up. No more long readings, we would do a five-card/fifteen-minute session for twenty-five dollars. We were changing from *Cheers* to Olive Garden.

It felt strange not to see Jimmy at the B & G. With my puncheon for ghost visits, I half expected to find him waiting for me with his hands full of curly fries.

My first client was a weeping teenage girl. Yes, if she saw her boyfriend kissing another girl under the bleachers he cheated on her. No, she was not going to marry him. Yes, she needed to finish high school before she ran off to join the Peace Corps, a convent, or the circus. No, she would not win the lottery this week. I didn't even bother to point out she was too young to be playing.

I felt an ethical responsibility to interpret the information I gathered in a kind and respectful manner. Most people found their way to where they need to be, even if they didn't want to go there. For the next thirty minutes, we talked and shared my plate of "to die for" lasagna. She left a tip for Laura, but I couldn't charge her. She told me the answers to each of her questions before I told her mine. All she really needed was someone to listen. I didn't care that it went over the new time limit.

The rest of the evening passed without event, four easy-peasy readings with no disasters in sight. Toward closing an elderly lady wheeled her walker over to my table, and did what Mom had called a "controlled crash" into the chair across from me.

"Honey, I need you to get a message to my dead husband."

I started to protest, but before I could get a word of explanation out, the little old woman pulled out a worn black and white picture, some sort of a naval war medal, a turquoise comb, matching wedding rings, and a rusty horseshoe from the *Mary Poppins* carpetbag tied to her walker. She scattered the bits amongst my own tabletop trophies.

"As I said, hon, I want you to talk to my Jo-jo for me. My name is Cecelia Ray. I noticed you sneak in a shot of Crown now and again, but I thought might you enjoy the ritual of absinthe. I got permission from Our Lady of the Boat to bring it in for you."

Claire as sainted lady of the seas? I giggled. Something seemed familiar about this elderly woman in front of me, but I couldn't figure it.

"Miss Cecelia Ray, you're not going to have me seeing

the green faeries, are you?"

"This bottle was distilled in France. I smuggled it in," she whispered in a conspiratorial voice. "I think the wormwood has been purified almost to the point of impotency, but you never know." Cecelia Ray shook the bottle. "Shall we find out together?"

Laura came to our table, and set down two uniquely shaped glasses, two cubes of sugar and a sterling silver slotted spoon.

"I've heard stories about the writers and artists that used this drink in days . . ."

"Long gone," Cecelia Ray finished my sentence.

"For pleasure," I added.

"For inspiration."

"For decadence and despair."

I wasn't sure how the fabled tincture would affect me tonight. I could tell from the fluidness of her actions that this was not Cecelia Ray's first wormwood encounter. She attended to pouring with a practiced grace in her movement. My morals nagged me tonight. I wanted to taste the liquor, but not under false expectations. Cecelia Ray began by reciting a Wiccan blessing.

"May kindness from my heart touch yours."

Death By Catgut

The opaque green fluid swirled through the sugar cubes and into the glasses. It smelled bittersweet and absolutely inviting. When she finished the greeting, she offered me a glass.

"And be returned from mine," I answered.

She smiled demurely, but I saw depth of personality and experience behind her old, honey-amber colored eyes.

"Miss Cecelia Ray, I appreciate this gesture, but I have to be honest with you. The term psychic is a rather general term for people like me who gather or give information . . . by means of . . . other than normal communication channels. You said you want to get a message to your late husband. A medium is better suited to translate between the living and the dead. That's the kind of person you want to talk to. Me, I work mostly with energy fields. I don't go too deep into anyone's past."

Except my own.

She concentrated on our drinks. I rambled on.

"My abilities focus on possibilities. That knowledge mixed with common sense most often helps folks figure out their own situation."

"You are a charlatan?"

That question stopped me in my tracks. "No. The cards are an effect. I listen to people, and I point out options when someone doesn't believe they have any. I provide a legitimate service."

"That's nice, dear. Sip this slowly." Cecelia Ray saluted me. "Let me explain something, child." She finished her drink, not following her own advice. "There are what I describe as fixed points in time and space, moments that cannot be changed, but most of what we human beings deal with is what I call fluid fate."

"Fluid fate." I liked the sound of that as I repeated it. "And . . ."

"We cannot control all our experiences. That's an illusion we hold to for comfort. We can, however, manage our responses." she sighed. "Another?"

"Thank you, no. I have the feeling I may need my wits about me for the rest of this conversation."

"I've discovered my life full of 'if/then' events. If I choose this, then that will happen. If I choose that, then this will happen."

"I changed my mind. Will Splenda do?" I ripped open a packet, dumped it into my glass and poured smoky green liquid on top. "What's your message?"

"Tell Jo-jo, I won't be joining him any time soon."

"Places to go, people to meet."

"Sarcasm doesn't suit you," she interrupted my tangent.

"I've been told that. I'm sorry. What was the message again?"

"I changed my mind."

"Why don't you tell him yourself?"

"Not everyone jumps the veil as easily as you." She wobbled to a stand. "And with this choice, I change my fate. I give over my 'expiration date' to God."

It may have only been me, but it felt like the restaurant took a breath. I witnessed a being create a fixed moment in time and space, her decision to live.

"What about your . . ." I motioned to her trinkets on my table, "memorabilia?"

"Bits and pieces of a broken life that I don't need anymore, but you might." She rose, leaving the absinthe behind, and wheeled herself and her walker out of the door.

Jerri Ann raced in, almost knocking Cecelia Ray over. The younger woman paled at the sight of the teetering elder. There was symmetry to my evening. A crying teen trying to begin the night, a crying post teen trying to fix her life at the close of business, with a crazy old lady in the middle talking about fluid fate. A cube of sugar wasn't going to sweeten this. I grabbed for the bottle of green insight and took a raw swallow.

Naomi Patterson

Bits and Pieces

"**He**'s gonna kill you," Jerri Ann blurted out.

Crap, crap, crap, what have I done now? "Ah, what? Whom are you talking about?" I mumbled as she plopped down in an agitated state of frenzy. I noticed she had changed her shoes to ballet slipper-style flats. *Easier to run in?*

"You. Joey. He's gonna kill you. I didn't mean anything by it, Nan. Really I didn't."

"Slow down. What are you talking about?"

She took a breath. I signaled to Laura to bring her a brew.

"I told Joey about our conversation. He called you a meddling, busybody bitch."

"I've been called worse."

"He said you have no business saying the things you say, and that he was going to shut you up, forever."

My recent change away from suicide maven made the

278

thought of dying at someone else's hand a disconcerting notion. *To my own amazement, now I want to live.*

"He's a mean drunk and not much better sober," Jerri Ann confessed.

I downplayed the drama. "Joseph is a bit of a hothead. He was blowing off steam."

"No." Jerri Ann dropped her voice. "You don't understand what he's capable of."

Laura handed Jerri Ann a beer. I pulled out three dollars, but Laura waved it away. Jerri Ann lowered her eyes to my table. Her gaze lingered on the turquoise colored comb.

"Joey has one of those awful colored combs. It's some kind of family joke. I didn't think it was going to be like this."

"It?"

She wiggled in her chair, "Being with Joey. Living in this place. Life!"

"None of us ever do."

"Watch your back." Jerri Ann chugged her brew and wobbled out. It wasn't her first beer of the night.

Claire closed the restaurant and brought a glass for herself to my table. "Share!" she said producing a hand full of sugar cubes.

I handed her the bottle of absinthe.

"Any green winged creatures flying about?" she asked.

I shook my head no.

"Yeah, I never saw the green flash at sundown in the Keys either. Nice stories, though."

I fingered the forgotten treasures Cecelia Ray left behind. I picked up the comb and played it like a harmonica. Claire stomped her foot in time to my imaginary beat.

"Tweetle dee, Tweetle dum. Look out, murder, here we come."

"Sing it, sister," Claire exclaimed.

"Two down, one to go. Who done it, we don't know . . ."

"Don't give up your day jobs for a singing career." Ross laughed at us as he entered.

Claire choked on her drink, "Shit, Sheriff. You scared me."

"Lock your doors when you're here by yourself."

"I'm not here by myself." Claire repeatedly pointed in my direction.

"Cuz, you are really starting to creep me out. Sneaking around after dark-thirty."

"Wanted to check out how your *visit* with Jerri Ann and Joe went, off the record?"

"Which one?" asked Claire.

Death By Catgut

Ross arched an eyebrow. I offered him a green drink. He declined.

"Suit yourself. It's a once in a lifetime opportunity," I said. "Does a veiled death threat count, off the record?"

"Is that what Jerri Ann said to you?" asked Claire. "Someone needs to slap that girl stupid."

"Too late," Claire and I said together.

Ross coughed to cover a snicker. It was mean of us, however true.

"Don't shoot the messenger. She was repeating what Joe said. I hit a nerve this afternoon with my card reading."

I continued playing with Cecelia Ray's memorabilia. I noticed the medal was not US Navy, but from the Merchant Marines. That wing of service had the reputation of being "marine-lite," responsible for cargo and passenger transportation in times of peace. Tugboats and towboats came to mind. I fondled her wedding rings. No gold here. They were a kind of nut or gasket polished smooth, but dinged and dented from wear. I twisted the bands to the candlelight. Barely visible inside the names Josiah Daniel and Cecelia Ray Jackson were etched.

Just when I thought things couldn't get much weirder.

"Ah, Nan? Time to rejoin the pack, dear." Claire brought me out of my reverie.

"I think I met Grandma Jackson tonight."

"The old lady with the booze?"

I handed the rings to Ross and the marine-type medal to Claire.

"Bits and pieces of a life she no longer needed. That's what she said."

"So what?" asked Ross. "Husband dead, sons dead, one grandson dead and the other one a pretty good bet for cousin-cide?"

"Cousin-cide . . . you made a joke. Not a good one, but I'll give you tiny points for the effort," I told Ross.

"Holy shit, JD had a blue-green comb like this one," Claire acknowledged. "When I teased him about being a girly-man, he told me it was a joke. Everyone in his family had one."

"Yup, family. Joe's got one, and my guess is Jimmy did too."

"If Miss Cecelia Ray is part of the long-lost members of the Jackson clan, why wait until now to come forward? And why come in here and not go to the sheriff?" asked Claire.

"Maybe she didn't get the information until too late, didn't care, didn't have the heart to deal with it all," I offered. "Wait. She was here. She was here at the memorial service."

"The little ol' lady in the booth," Claire's memory

confirmed mine.

"Yeah, she sat right there." I pointed to the spot. "Cuz, you're being awfully quiet."

"Thinking on whether or not I need to take you two into custody."

"I beg your pardon," sputtered Claire.

Ross held up his hands in defense. "Protective custody. I can't wait for the DNA to come back proving JD was Joe's father. And that really doesn't matter. But it's time to bring Joe and Jerri Ann in for questioning."

"I understand the need to question those two," I said, "but what are you going to ask 'em? Talk to Grandma lately?"

"Nope. I'm going to ask them if they killed Jimmy and JD. Joe is strong and mean enough to do it. Jerri Ann is gullible enough to help him. If so, they tried to frame Claire, in case she and JD pillow-talked about the family. And Jerri Ann did threaten you tonight."

"Well, it wasn't so much a real death threat, as a . . ."

"You sure about that, are you?" Ross snapped at me. "Lock up, Miss Claire. Nan grab your stuff."

"You are not going to put us in jail overnight," declared Claire. "I've seen the inside of a cell, and I will not 'go gentle into that good night.' If you get my drift?"

"Yes, ma'am. But I will drive you both to Hilltop, and put you under lock and key with Harvey."

"Chauvinist," I accused.

"No, pragmatist. If Joe and Jerri Ann try something before I can round them up and bring them in, it's three against two, odds in your favor. Let's go, ladies."

To my cousin's surprise we didn't argue.

#

At home in the wee hours of the morn, Harvey and Claire cuddled on a sleeping bag pallet in front of our newly refurbished and working fireplace in the downstairs parlor. We had the emotional need to huddle. Mutt and a few of our cats lay about the room as I paced. Max paddy-pawed in carrying what I thought to be a large rat. I was ready to "eak" when the small black form mewed. The kitten started yowling the moment the big guy dropped his tiny, cat-spit-covered body at my feet. Several of the other kitties came to investigate and comfort.

Uh-oh, number sixteen. What kind of crazy comes after daffy-doodles?

I knew we had another house member the moment he looked up at me with those emerald green eyes. He was barely big enough to be weaned, but his paws were ginormous. When I asked Max where he found the kitten, he ignored me. His job was done.

Claire and I brought Harv up to speed on the evening's events. Claire kept staring at the old photo Cecelia Ray left behind, while Harv examined the merchant marine medal. My energy spent, I settled back in a beanbag chair that I might need help getting out of. Grown-up furniture was on our new list.

"The more I look at this picture, the more I see a family resemblance," Claire said.

"I wish the photo were in color." I speculated, "The boys got their eye color from grandma."

Harvey pondered, "So, Cecelia Ray Jackson comes back from her own grave to attend the memorial service her son and grandson. She wanders into the bar to drop these trinkets on your table for what purpose?"

"Carill's Fine Dinning Establishment, if you please," interrupted Claire. "We are no longer a bar and grill."

"Yes." He kissed her cheek and refocused on the trinkets. "Why this stuff? Why now?"

"Timing?" I shrugged. "Never been my strong suit. My guess is Miss Cecelia Ray Jackson came as soon as she could, and did what she could to help us sort out her family debacle without being stuck in the mire, legally or emotionally. I think she left before Jimmy and Joe were born. I don't remember her at all. Do you?"

Harvey shook his head. "The Jackson wives don't stick around long."

"That's another story," Claire said.

"We did have the 'raise a few in honor and adieu' at your fine dining establishment." I winked at Claire. "A sitting psychic is an easy target. Any other night it would have been Judy at the table. Bringing the absinthe made us focus on the gift more than her."

"I did get a call at the bar yesterday asking if a present for the psychic would be all right, but the lady didn't use your name or give hers. I told her 'fine by me'."

"Maybe it wasn't me specifically she needed." I searched my memory for an instant replay. "But guys, she made me feel like she knew me. She talked about if/then clauses, life choices, expiration dates, fate."

"Maybe she recognized a kindred spirit." Claire comforted me.

"Maybe she knew my grandmother? And, I do happen to come with the added benefit of a family member in law enforcement."

"Sleep now, rally round the sheriff in the morning," suggested Harvey. "Nan, you got a postcard from Zach today.

It's on the kitchen counter."

"My brother say anything interesting?"

Harvey yawned. "Zach said, you needed to see him."

"Did he happen to mention when or why?"

"Nope."

We all bunked down looking like a summer camp for cats. Whisper, our newest addition snuggled in to nurse on my little finger while Punkin licked his ears. The room filled with soft sounds of rhythmic breathing.

Cat's In The Cradle

Ross called first thing the next morning to tell Harvey he could release Claire and me from house arrest, and that he had Joe and Jerri Ann in custody. Everyone had places to go and things to do except me. I read the postcard from my brother, and taped it up on the fridge. Zach actually added a return address in the corner, something he'd never included before. He was living in Sonoma Valley, and working as a wine sommelier rather than grape picker. He had a regular job, an apartment, a girlfriend, and felt his little sister needed to come see him. He gave me an open invitation and promised to pay for an airline ticket or gas.

Maybe a change of scenery would be good for me?

#

The Angel Falls jail had two cells, a unisex bathroom, the sheriff's office, a larger room with maps and charts of local waters on the wall. That space functioned as a combination situation-conference-interrogation room. The waiting area was a converted storefront taken over when the town council voted to expand the office. There was enough space for a couple of benches and a secretarial desk, but not enough money to keep someone sitting there. Deputy Ron did double duty answering the phone when he wasn't cruising the farm-to-market roads or serving warrants.

The sheriff wore cowboy boots, pressed jeans and a crisp white shirt that made the six-pointed, silver star over his heart stand out. It bothered me that it looked a lot more like a target than a badge of duty and honor. The straw cowboy hat he wore in the spring set on its top so as not to mess the brim shape he had carefully crafted for fit and style.

Upside-down like that, it begs for a pot plant. A small Northfork pine.

"Morning," I waltzed in, sans witchy regalia.

"Morning."

I poured myself coffee in his cup. My cousin shuffled some papers and nodded his head toward his office. I followed like I was going to the principal's office.

Trying to be upbeat I offered, "I got a postcard from Zachary."

"He sign it with a purple thumbprint?"

"Always. He wants to see me."

"Uhm." Ross changed the subject. "You're here early."

"True. I want to know how all this comes out."

"You don't already?" he teased.

"Don't spread this around, because it wouldn't be good for my Friday night business, but since I decided to stay on this side of the 'wee thin veil,' my insight has suffered. The dragons aren't singing so loudly any more. If you know what I mean?"

"Is that such a bad thing?"

I blew a long breath through puckered lips. "I suppose it depends on how I define myself: senile soothsayer, card-reading quack, middle-aged maven of mayhem, inconsequential vet assistant."

"How about dear friend, loved family member, community activist?"

"Thank you."

"You bring the stuff?"

"Yup." I tossed him the paper bag.

"We don't have a two-way mirror here, and I can't have you sit in on the interrogation. I have to digitally record everything. I can't have you even sit in as a secretary. I can leave the door cracked, and you can eavesdrop. We have to wait until Ron gets back from his morning rounds to begin. He works all the camera equipment."

"Who you going to talk to first?"

"I think Joe. He's angry, but I don't think he's going to say anything to incriminate himself. He'll lawyer up. But while he's waiting for his due process, I can bring Jerri Ann in. She's the weakest link in this whole thing."

"Yeah, but is she more afraid of Joe or you?"

"We'll find out."

"Crap, you don't have them in there together do you?"

He gave me the stare. "Jerri Ann is offsite, and Snookie is babysitting."

"Snookie? Why did you deputize a retired RN-Health store owner and not me?"

Damn, two stares in a row. I raised my hands in surrender.

I spent the next twenty minutes filing my nails while Ross did office stuff. About the time my butt fell asleep, Ron came back and set up everything in the other room.

"We're ready for him, boss," Ron announced.

Joe remained defiant as expected. He rattled his handcuffs at me when he crossed the hall. I smiled ever so sweetly, waved bye-bye and pretended to leave. Ross left the door cracked for me to see and hear. Joe propped his boots up on the table. Through my hole I watched my cousin work.

"You gonna pay me for lost income while I'm sitting here, and the station is closed?" Joe asked.

Ross stayed silent. Standing above the suspect, my cousin cut an imposing figure. He knocked Joe's muddy boots off the table. Joe sat up to avoid tumbling out of his chair.

"This is stupid, Sheriff."

Without speaking Ross set the paper bag I had brought him in front of Joe, and waited. Unnerving quiet. I supposed that was the point.

"What's this all about?" Joe asked. His voice edged more toward nervous than angry.

Ross reached in the bag and dropped the merchant marine medal Cecelia Ray left behind on the table. It spun like a top before it clattered to a stop.

"Mr. Jackson, this is about a family injustice, and some boyhood jealousies that turned into murder."

Joe snorted his derision.

"Your grandmother dropped this by." Ross fingered the medal.

"My grandmother is dead. My whole family is dead. I'm the last of my kind."

"That's an incorrect assumption. I guess a double

homicide in her family was more than Grandma Jackson could bear. She's back in Angel Falls, and she had a few interesting things to say about your family."

"What the hell are you yammering about?"

Ross took out a turquoise comb and laid it next to the medal. Joe stilled. Ross pulled out Jimmy's old baseball cap and shaped the brim. Joe shifted in his chair.

"Jimmy was fond of this hat. He was wearing it the night you killed him. You were wearing it the night you killed your father."

"My father?"

"Yes, JD was your daddy. Josiah Daniel Jackson, Junior. And both times you were looking for this." Ross pulled out a crumpled, stained piece of old paper.

"What's that shit?"

"This, this is the deed to the Jackson Family Gas Station. You thought Jimmy kept it folded up in his hat, and you killed him for it. But what you needed, Mr. Jackson, was this." Ross opened an official looking file folder. "This is your Grandfather's Last Will and Testament. It names your father, not Jimmy's dad as sole beneficiary. You thought when you got rid of your cousin you'd take over the station. Then Junior announced his identity, and you thought you'd be stepped over, forgotten again. So you killed him."

"This is bullshit. You hear me? This is bullshit. You and that crazy, old witch cousin of yours are making this up. I want a lawyer!"

With those last four words spoken, Ross told Ron to stop the video. The deputy escorted Joe back to his cell. They couldn't ask any more questions. Jerri Ann came next. Ross and Snookie walked her by the cells before escorting her to the interrogation room.

"Joey?" Jerri Ann squeaked.

"You keep your mouth shut, bitch."

Snookie shut the hallway door toward the cells, eliminating their chance to hear each other. Snookie saw me, and winked as she maneuvered Jerri Ann into her seat. Ross didn't have any female officers. I knew Snookie helped out when needed. She looked good in her white shirt, jean skirt, grey alligator cowgirl boots and shiny badge (her version of the non-uniform Ross and Ron wore). I wasn't really jealous. I didn't have the patience to help out in the office, and babysitting a suspect was way beyond my abilities.

Cecelia Ray and Jimmy's belongings lay arranged on the table along with the tea-stained documents. I'd visually enhanced the papers to age them.

Death By Catgut

A little Earl Grey goes a long way.

I bounced a copy of the deed around in the dryer with my tennis shoes to soften the edges. I wasn't sure how Ross came up with Gramps Jackson's Will. I never found one in the county records. Maybe he bounced some papers around in his dryer too. Not sure how the court would feel about our visual aids. I hoped for a confession.

Ross went through the same spiel with Jerri Ann, but after he mentioned the Last Will and Testament he added a twist. "Your companion, Miss Stevens, has asked for a lawyer. He's giving you up."

"Joey, wouldn't do that. He loves me."

At that I came out of hiding, but not enough to be on camera. "Jerri Ann, Joe didn't give you up, he sent you down the river!" I screamed at her. "Girl, he didn't ask for a lawyer to protect you. He's covering his own ass. He's going for a deal where he tells the District Attorney it was your idea to kill Jimmy and JD for the money. You're the one wearing diamonds. He sold you out."

Jerri Ann jumped to her feet to bolt, but had no way out. Ross jerked his head toward Snookie and then at me. Snookie gently pushed me out of the room.

Calmer now, I called over my shoulder, "You are going

to die for his crimes. Remember the card castle we built? Joe's the one betraying you."

Jerri Ann looked like I had sucked the breath out of her, a cat in the cradle. It was an old superstition wrongly interpreted. Cats didn't steal life from sleeping children, but rather protected them by sleeping in their cribs to keep them warm. I wondered why I was trying to help Jerri Ann.

I stopped letting Snookie push me out of the room and turned to look Jerri Ann straight in her eyes. "You don't owe that man the rest of your life," I said with an eerie calmness. I wasn't sure if it was for her benefit or mine. Maybe both.

"Nan, get the hell out of here," shouted Ross.

Once out of the room, I slumped down the wall to sit on the floor. Snookie shut the door.

"Miss Stevens, sit down!" Ross commanded.

"Oh, God . . . oh God. Is Nan right? Am I gonna die?" Jerri Ann started screaming. "It was an accident. Joey didn't mean to kill Jimmy. He said we were going to scare him. A joke, you know, all in fun, like."

Ross remained stern. "Miss Stevens, you have been advised of your rights. Do you understand what you are saying?"

"Yes," she sobbed. "Sheriff, it wasn't my idea, I swear.

Joe, he said that Jimmy stole his family treasure map, and we were going to get it back. I thought he meant we were going on a scavenger hunt. It sounded like fun, you know, pirates and all, but he meant that damn gas station. That dirty, smelly, greasy, God-forsaken gas station."

Damn pirates.

"Miss Stevens, you are confessing to murder."

"Oh no, Sheriff. Joey killed him. Joey killed them both. I just helped him move the body."

What a letdown. I'm not sure what I expected, but it wasn't what I felt. Cain and Abel was one of the oldest stories in the world.

You have something I want . . . I'll kill you for it.

"Miss Stevens, why did you kill Joe's father?"

"What are you talking about?" she sobbed.

"JD. JD was Joe's father, Josiah Daniel Jackson, Junior."

"His father? I'm sorry. I didn't know. I didn't know. Joe said that the cook guy was stalking him. He said he was afraid that JD would hurt me."

"I'm sure Joe said a lot of things." Ross's voice changed to consoling, "Why don't you tell me what happened in your own words?"

When Jerri Ann spoke, her voice was soft. I put my ear

297

at the door to listen.

"Joe woke me up about midnight, and said he wanted to give his cousin a scare. He told me to dress up like a zombie, you know, greyish make up and tattered clothes. Joey drove me up to the hills, and told me he was going to chase Jimmy into the woods. When his cousin came my way, I was to jump out from behind this special tree and scare him."

"And you did this?" asked Ross.

"No. They never showed up. I got tired of waiting and left. It was dark. I was cold. It started raining, so I went home. My feet hurt. I must have walked miles. I was mad a Joey for leaving me out there. I didn't find out about Jimmy until the next week like everybody else. When I asked Joey about it, he said that his cousin tripped and rolled down a hill."

"That's all well and good, but Miss Stevens we found Jimmy's body up on the hillside. His neck had been broken and soft parts of his body had been eaten away by coyotes. Broken neck and eaten," he repeated. "Do you want me to show you the crime scene photos? Or can you imagine it for yourself?"

Jerri Ann started blubbering and babbling at the same time. "I didn't do it. I didn't know."

"But you did know, and you said nothing. Then you helped Joe kill his father and move the body into Miss

McCarthy's house."

"Joe said that sailor-bitch was blackmailing him, and he had to make JD and her leave us alone."

"JD left town. He wasn't a threat," Ross countered.

"He came back by the gas station. We were already closed. I heard them arguing out in the garage. I think Joey hit him in the head with a tire iron, but I didn't see it. Joe had me drive the pickup over to Claire's house."

"And you helped him carry the body inside."

"No, honest, Sheriff."

"Miss Stevens, do not use that word with me. Honest is not a word you understand. How did you cover up dragging the body in?"

"Joey is real strong when he's excited."

"Jerri Ann Stevens," Ross used her full name.

I cringed for her.

"Swiffer Sweeper," she admitted. "I roughed the rug up with Claire's sweeper thingy. You know, not enough to make it look cleaned up."

I can hear the new product jingle already: "Makes hiding a body easier."

"Miss Stevens, I'm charging you as an accessory to murder."

"What if I testify against Joe? Do I get a deal?"

Amazing. Murder and betrayal in less than ten minutes. This could be a new reality show.

Bile rose in my throat. On TV once the villains confess, everyone's satisfied, and the screen fades to black. On *Criminal Minds,* the good guys fly home on their private jet while the voice-over quotes words of wisdom, and the viewer sleeps better knowing the world has been saved from one more serial killer. I think real-life peace officers spend more time trying to rinse the memories from their minds at a bar rather than testifying before one.

I need a drink or three.

Death By Catgut

Escape Claws

The "For Sale" sign disappeared from the front door of Carill's. I walked into the B & G to watch Claire and Glen shaking hands. Claire folded up some papers and waved at me.

"Come on in Nan, and have your last drink on the house."

"In that case, make mine a double."

Glen walked behind the counter, and poured us all a tall shot of Crown.

"To the worst of 'em gone before us," Claire said for the last time in her bar.

I answered her for the first time in hope, "And to the best of 'em yet to come."

"Good days, better nights," added Glen with a wink.

I sipped slowly as Claire and Glen told me of their deal. Glen bought the place. Claire would stay on as manager for a couple of months to make the paperwork transition easier. When

I thought about it, the transformation had taken place already. It wasn't the real tablecloths and the refined menu. The Bar and Grill changed. The town changed. I changed.

Glen started to speak, but I stopped him.

"No worries. I'm ready to put my Granny's cards in a drawer for a while."

"I told you she would know," Claire eyeballed Glen.

He bowed and meandered back to the kitchen, leaving us to finish our drinks in private. I told her what I could about Joe and Jerri Ann without crossing confidences.

"See you this evening," she said as I got up to leave.

"Oh?"

"Hey, I'm a *day* manager now, and Harvey's cooking."

#

Harvey already knew about the sale, Claire already knew about Joe and Jerri Ann, but neither of them knew about me leaving. I didn't give voice to my idea until after dinner. We sat on the back porch finishing a fruity dessert. Punkin shared my lap with Whisper. Too much wine made me blurt it out.

"I think Claire should become a third partner here, with all three of our names on the deed, and we should turn Hilltop into a pet friendly Bed and Breakfast. The town is growing, tourist trade is picking up. It feels like the right time to do this."

302

Death By Catgut

The proverbial shit-eating grin crept across Harvey's face. He went into the house and returned with blueprints.

"There's space for a small library-slash-sitting room," he offered.

"An art gallery entranceway and a tea patio," Claire opened her arms to embrace our surroundings. "Nannie, I got a good deal on the bar. That money, along with a portion of Harv's savings, and a lot of elbow grease, and we can have this place ready for the fall season."

"What about your, um, studio?" I asked Harvey, gesturing to the third floor.

"Being remodeled into a luxury apartment for you with a plant-slash-cat terrace." He pointed to the blueprints.

"Stop saying 'slash'," I pleaded. "And the non-living critters?"

"All our stuffed beasties are being donated to the education outreach program over in Zoerne. It's time for me to focus on the living."

Yes, time for us all.

"We'll have to update the kitchen, add in more bathrooms, and there will be permits and paperwork out the wazoo to complete. We'll have to take classes in food prep and maybe even get a liquor license. Claire knows how to do all that . . . I mean, we haven't thought or talked all this out."

"Where are you and Claire going to live?" When they didn't answer, I gave them my "oh please" expression. I knew they were headed for forever before they did.

Harvey actually blushed. "We have plans to build two or three cottages hidden away in our 'woods,' once I graduate from vet school, or as the B & B grows. Until then, we'll stay at Claire's house during the remodel or take over one of the rooms on the second floor."

"What about adding on a suite over here, where the old waterwheel is?" I pointed to the empty space on the blueprint.

"We didn't know how you'd take all this, Nan," admitted Claire.

"I'm taking it fine. I think this is wonderful, but there is one more thing. I don't want this to sound bad . . . I'm leaving."

"What?" They said in tandem.

Harvey started stammering about how this was only an idea, that nothing needed to change. Claire started crying.

"Wait, wait guys. That's what I mean, but not how I mean it. You two are my life. And, not but, and it's time for all of us to move forward. The Bed and Breakfast is a great plan."

Claire came over and wrapped her arms around me.

I kissed the top of her head. "The changes we are all

making are healthy. Remember the postcard I got from Zach? I'm not supposed to tell, but he got a girl knocked up and he needs me . . . You should see the expression on your faces. Oh, come on guys it's a joke. Z-man is older than us. But he does need some brother-sister bonding time. I've never seen the California wine country. I want to go visit him."

Claire squeezed my hand and I reassured her. "Don't worry, I'll be back. You can't get rid of me that easy."

"Nan, take out your dragons," pleaded Harvey.

"I don't know if they'll sing to me or not." I pulled the Tarot cards from my pocket. I shuffled them, cut them, flipped the first card on top of the blueprints, and smiled.

#

The old VW was not up to the task of a cross-country trip. The newly incorporated Angel Falls Bed and Breakfast purchased a van for customer pickup from the Zoerne airport, for grocery runs, for me to go to California in, etc., etc., etc. We settled on "Angel Falls" instead of Hilltop B & B, so we'd be the first listed in the phone book. We had options to explore as we developed our business plan.

Of course, we will be a pet friendly establishment.

My boss at the vet clinic, Dr. Word, said she'd miss me, but she was excited about Harvey going back to school. He'd make a good addition to her practice when he graduated. She promised I'd have a job whenever I wanted it.

I felt guilty running out on the work that would take place in the next several months, both at the vet office and our home, but it was important for my two best friends to have some "alone time" at this stage in their relationship. Important for me, too.

My suitcases were packed. Ross and his family made me a picnic basket. Harvey and Claire got me an iPhone to match theirs as a bon voyage present. And, Claire's niece put a million apps on it for me.

I know how to use the phone and the map thingy.

Laura did get me started with DragonVale. Breeding and growing and playing with dragons was an app made for me. I had FaceTime too. I liked the idea of being able to see all the kitties when I called home to talk with Harvey and Claire. Punkin and our newest kitten, Whisper, were travelling with me. They were crated and waiting in the van. It was time to go. I hugged Harvey and Claire for the third time. Claire offered me my flask. I shook my head, no thanks.

Breathe, Nannie. Put one foot in front of the other.

I climbed in the van and immediately opened Punkin's cage. She jumped in my lap and head-butted the window. I kissed my fingers and pressed them to the window as well.

"You've got the map, and you've got your phone, and you've got the map on the phone?" asked Harvey.

"Yes, yes and yes," I replied.

"Safe sailing," whispered Claire.

As I rolled down our little driveway, the mandolin solo from Rascal Flatts's "I'm Moving On" rose up from the new stereo system. I looked in the rearview mirror. Max and Cricket stood vigil on the widow's walk. There were spots of color throughout the yard where our other kitties played. Mittens and Marmalade rounded the corner and pounced on Mutt. Claire and Harvey held each other around the waist and waved.

"Call every night when you stop, and when you get to Zach's," Claire instructed. "Promise?"

"Promise," I swore, even though she couldn't hear the words.

"Hey," Harvey yelled after me, "if you're not back by Halloween, I'm getting a dog."

Mutt shook off his kitties and chased the van down the driveway, barking his goodbye.

My smile returned beneath my tears as I thought, "We already have one."

Naomi Patterson

About the Author

Naomi "Nome" Patterson was born in Verdun, France, the second daughter to George and Velma Patterson, a military family. After completing graduate school at UT in Austin, Texas, Naomi lectured a year at Baylor University. For the next twenty-five years she worked on-staff or freelance for advertising agencies, video production companies and independent national corporations as a writer, producer and director based out of Dallas and Houston.

Family health issues brought her to New Braunfels, Texas, in 2002. While caring for her mother, she worked at the public library, contracted freelance corporate writing jobs, focused on her creative writing and functioned as an Associate Producer and Assistant Director on a couple of independent Texas-based feature films.

She was a charter member of the New Braunfels Writer's Guild, and is active with River City Ink – a Fiction Writers Group. Naomi's personal interests include reading, writing, modeling in costume for the New Braunfels Art League, travel, gardening, hiking in the woods, snow skiing and yoga. She continues to live in New Braunfels with three cats.